E

MW01131320

Mistress to the Beast

By

Eve Vaughn

Dedication

To Wanda and Shayna for always holding it down for me and to all my readers for your continued support.

This is a work of fiction. Names, characters, places, and incidents are products of the author's imagination or are used fictitiously and are not to be construed as real. Any resemblance to actual events, locales, organizations, or persons living or dead is entirely coincidental.

All trademarks, service marks, registered service marks are the property of their respective owners and are used herein for identification purposes only.

Chapter One

"He can't do this to you! We'll fight him and his damn company—if that's what needs to be done, but Saunders will remain in business!" Lila slammed her fist on the dinner table, making the plates and utensils clatter against it.

Jesse Saunders wagged his finger from side to side with a shake of his head. "Watch your language, young lady."

Even at twenty-seven, Lila had to censor her words around her father, who thought it unladylike for women to swear. Lately, she'd been doing a lot of it.

"I'm sorry, Dad, but we can't sit back and watch everything you've worked so hard to build be destroyed by some reclusive property developer. This is your livelihood and our home." Tears stung the backs of her eyes as she blinked them away. It didn't seem fair they should lose everything on some rich man's whim.

"Dad, there has to be something we can do to stop them. They can't just take our home like this! Saunders is your life." She wiped away an angry tear that had escaped the corner of her eye. Lila didn't want to break down in front of her father, especially when he was probably trying to stay strong for her. But emotion threatened to overwhelm her.

Jesse pushed his half-eaten dinner away and placed his head in his hands. "You're right. It's my life, not yours, and I've depended on you for far too long."

Lila's breath caught in her throat. Surely he wasn't thinking of giving up. "What are you trying to say, Dad?"

Her father lifted his head with the suspicious sheen of tears glistening in his eyes. "Baby, this is my battle to fight. Not yours. I'm guilty of leaning on you a lot more than I should have. I ought to be the one taking care of you, not the other way around."

She waved her hand dismissively. "Don't be ridiculous. If you can't count on family, who else can you depend on? I'm not doing anything I don't want to do."

"Lila, your heart is in the right place, but maybe it's time to wave the white flag. I'm an old man, and although there's nothing I'd like more than to keep the shop running until the day I die, I don't think I can do it on my own *and* fight Ramsey's."

Lila reached across the table and grasped her father's hand in earnest. "Daddy, you have me."

"And that's the problem," he sighed.

She wasn't sure whether to be hurt or angry at his comment. "Why is my being here a problem?"

He held up his hand. "That came out wrong."

"How else am I supposed to take it when you imply you don't need me, that you don't want me around?"

Jesse shook his head vehemently. "Baby girl, I'll always need you, but like I said, I can't keep leaning on you so much. You're a young, beautiful woman—exceptionally so."

Lila snorted, rolling her eyes. "Don't start that again."

"It's true."

"Fathers are supposed to say things like that to their daughters."

"I don't say anything I don't mean. I see the way men look at you. You're the image of your mother, God rest her soul. I used to wonder how a mug like me was lucky enough

5

to end up with an angel like my Eloise. She could have had anyone she wanted, you know, but for some reason she chose me."

A smile touched Lila's lips at the mention of her mother. She didn't remember her, but listening to her father reminisce made Lila feel closer to the woman who'd given her life. "Who are you trying to kid? You know you're a good-looking man. Mrs. Reyes comes by the shop every day and it's *not* to purchase milk. She has a crush on you." Lila giggled. There were quite a few women who gave him more than a second glance.

It was her father's turn to brush her comments aside. "Gloria is a nice lady. She's just looking for a little conversation."

"And a lot of you."

His lips firmed to one thin line as he shook his head. "You won't distract me from the topic. As I was saying, you're young and you should have a life of your own. You need to go back to your job, and find a nice young man to settle down with and give me some grandbabies."

Not this subject again. She should have known he would somehow steer the conversation in this direction. "Dad, I'm not interested in a relationship right now."

"Is that what you told that doctor you were seeing before I had my stroke?"

"That was nothing." The words came out a bit quicker than she intended.

Jesse lifted a brow, a knowing expression on his face. "You used to talk about him nonstop. I thought the two of you would get married."

"It wasn't serious, Dad." Lila couldn't quite meet his eyes. She didn't like lying to her dad. The truth was, Jason had asked her to marry him, but he couldn't understand why she had devoted so much of her time toward seeing her father get better.

"For God's sake, hire a private nurse! I'll pay for it. I don't think it's too much of me to expect my woman to spend some time with me," he'd said one day after another heated argument. Dr. Jason Orija wasn't used to being neglected by anyone and had no problem letting her know it.

"I'm a nurse. How could I put him in someone else's care when I'm quite capable of handling the job myself? I can't just ignore that fact. Besides, he's my father. I wouldn't expect you to abandon any of your family members if they required assistance. He needs me."

"I need you. You're going to have to make a decision: It's either me or him."

That ultimatum had been the final straw in a string of problems between the two of them. She did love Jason, or at least Lila thought she did, but how could she stay with someone who would force her to make such a choice? Lila realized then she couldn't. Jason hadn't taken it well, and not even a week later he was dating someone else, another nurse at the hospital. His actions had reaffirmed to Lila she'd made the right decision.

Jesse gave his daughter a long hard look. "You haven't lied to me since you were five years old and didn't want me to find out you'd broken your mother's favorite vase. You're not very good at lying, baby. I believe I'm doing the right thing."

Lila's heart beat a tattoo against her breast. "What? You've made a decision?"

"I'm going to sell. I won't let you waste your life taking care of me and fighting a war we can't win." Pain oozed from his voice, and his dark face looked gray all of a sudden.

Alarm shot through her. "Daddy, are you all right?" She rushed to his side.

"Don't you worry, child. It's just this old heart. Get me my pills and I'll be okay."

Lila wasted no time retrieving the prescription bottle from the medicine cabinet and a glass of water. On top of recovering from a stroke, he often suffered heart palpitations due to stress and unhealthy eating habits even though she tried her best to regulate the latter. The entire situation had taken its toll on him physically and mentally.

How could she let him give up something that meant so much to him? If only he didn't have the worry of what would happen to the shop, Lila was sure he'd get better. Selling the place would kill him, slowly but surely.

There had to be something she could do. Thus far, none of her efforts from writing Ramsey's, the local newspapers, and attending town council meetings, were getting her anywhere. Her one last resort would be to go to Ramsey's headquarters in Manhattan and demand a meeting with the CEO. Failure was not an option.

She needed to get out of their apartment for some fresh air. Seeing her father like this was heartbreaking and there was only so much she could take at the moment. "I can't argue with you if that's how you feel. I'm going to take a walk. Will you be okay?"

"I've been taking care of myself long before you were born. I'll be fine." Jesse waved her off.

Lila stood up and walked over to her father before giving him a kiss on the top of the head. She didn't take offense to his gruff tone. Her father's frustrations were understandable. "Okay, Daddy. I'll be back in a bit."

Once outside she breathed a huge sigh of relief. She didn't mind taking care of her father but sometimes she needed a break. Walking through the neighborhood she'd grown up in filled her with joy and sadness. She saw the street corner where she'd fallen off her bike when she was ten that had left a moon-shaped scar on her knee. Lila spied the water ice stand where she and her friends would eat cherry ices on a hot summer's day. The pizza shop and the two dollar movie theater were places she used to frequent when she was younger. Now they were all gone, bought out by some greedy land baron.

She tried not to cry as she strolled the blocks of places she used to frequent. Finally she ended up in the park where a few children played on the jungle gym. How could she give up the fight when this place meant so much to her? It was her home where she'd made so many memories. This place was worth fighting for and she refused to give up no matter what her father said.

Jarring rap music cut through her thoughts. Lila pulled her cell phone from her pocket and made a mental note to change her ring tone later that night. She'd chosen this particular song because it was popular at the time and had a catchy beat but the radio had played it so much, she was sick of hearing it. When she saw who the call was from, Lila was tempted not to answer, but knowing him he would keep calling until they finally spoke. It was better to get this over with and nip whatever he wanted in the bud.

"Jason, what do you want?"

The son of Nigerian immigrants who were both doctors, Jason was a respected trauma surgeon at the hospital Lila was a geriatric nurse. One of the youngest in his field, he was already one of the bests at what he did on the East Coast. Besides, being successful, he was incredibly good looking. All off the single women at the hospital gushed over how brilliant and handsome he was, and even a few of the married ones as well. The problem with Jason was that he knew it too and was more than a little arrogant. But Lila was so flattered that someone like him had chosen her when he had so many options that she'd decided to give him a chance. Besides, he could be quite charming when he wanted to be, not to mention he was a good lover. During the course of their relationship he'd swept Lila off her feet with his grand and romantic gestures, but looking back on that relationship, she saw that it had blinded her to the cracks in their foundation.

9

Jason loved talking about himself and rarely asked Lila about what she wanted. He often looked down on people he thought he was better than like people in the service industry. And he was inconsiderate of Lila's schedule. But whenever he'd do something romantic for her, she fooled herself into thinking that their problems were simply just regular couples' woes. When he'd made Lila choose between him and her father, the blinders had come off. Maybe she did need to date more according to her father, but when she didn't she had no plans of taking up with Jason again.

"And hello to you as well, Lila. How are you?"

She rolled her eyes, in no mood for pleasantries. "Again, I'm asking why you're calling. We're no longer dating and I'm on leave at the hospital so I can't think of one good reason why you haven't lost my number yet."

There was a pregnant pause on the other end of the line followed by a heavy sigh. "I would have hoped that you'd be happy to hear from me."

"Are you kidding me? When you gave me that ultimatum and I chose my father, it was over."

There was another long pause before Jason answered. "I was thinking…and maybe I was too hasty. I shouldn't have made you choose. We could have worked it out."

"I might have believed that a few months ago but the next week we broke up, you were dating Veronica." Veronica worked on the same floor at the hospital but in the oncology department. They had been friendly until Lila began dating Jason. After that, the other woman wouldn't acknowledge her presence. Since they hadn't been particularly close, Lila never gave it much thought until Jason went right to her after their breakup.

"That was a miscalculation. I thought you'd come to your senses and contact me."

"So basically you tried to make me jealous. I would think that playing those kinds of high school games would be beneath the dignity of the great Dr. Orija."

"Don't be like that, Lila. I admit I made a mistake. I understand that family is important and I shouldn't have put you in a position to choose."

"I'm glad you admit that, Jason, but I'm still not sure why you needed to call and tell me something I already know."

"You never used to be so disagreeable."

Lila was way too stressed to put up with his bullshit. "I used to be a lot of things, Jason. Can you get to the point?"

"You're not making this easy for me. I don't make a habit of chasing women because truthfully, I can have any woman I want and we both know that. But I don't want just any woman. I want you. You're beautiful, accomplished even though you're just a nurse but that doesn't matter. You can always back to school and get your MSN. Besides that, my parents like you and you know how to handle yourself in a social setting."

"I see." Lila regretted the two years they'd dated because she could never get them back. In his righteous conceit he showed her exactly why she made the right decision to dump him. "So I guess you weren't able to mold Veronica in to the image of the perfect woman."

"Veronica comes from a different background. She's a little rough around the edges if you know what I mean."

"No actually I don't, why don't you tell me, Jason." Lila did know what he was getting at but she wanted to know if he'd says the words out loud.

"Let's just say that you can take the girl from streets, but you can't take the streets from the girl."

"Wow. How did it take me so long notice what a pompous asshole you are?"

"Excuse me?"

"Oh, you're excused, from this conversation and from out of my life." And with that, she pressed the end button on her phone and turned it to silent. Seconds later it vibrated signaling that she had another call. It was probably Jason, incredulous that Lila actually had the audacity to hang up on him.

She couldn't let his feelings bother her right now because she had far more important things to worry about. And her number one priority was saving her father's store.

Later that night, after she'd done the cleaning up and her father was in bed, Lila flopped on the couch from exhaustion. Was it already three years since they'd received that damned letter, an offer to purchase the building they lived in? The problem being, it wasn't only their home, but where her father's business was housed. Shortly afterwards, her father suffered his stroke. Lila had taken leave from her position as a geriatric nurse to assist during her father's recovery and rehabilitation, as well as manage the store while dealing with a property developer.

After refusing to sell out for months, Lila learned the city was interested in purchasing their property under eminent domain. Apparently the powers that be at Ramsey's had friends in high places. If the city bought their home, they could sell it for as much—or as little—to Ramsey's as they wanted to. From that point on, her father seemed to age before her very eyes.

She picked up one of the newspapers she'd saved. It was months old, but it had an article within in it that talked of the plans for the shopping center and all the stores that would be included—in her neighborhood. Who were they kidding? Didn't they realize people had lost their homes and businesses in order for this waste of mortar to be built? She scanned the rest of the article which discussed the developers of the project and the head man himself, Hunter Jamison.

Dubbed "the Beast" for his aggressive business tactics, he'd taken over the nearly bankrupt Ramsey's over ten years ago and turned it into one of the largest companies of its kind in the country. The paper contained an earlier picture of him and he looked every bit the Viking he was said to be descended from. Larger than life in the photograph, with his broad shoulders and barrel-sized chest, he seemed more suited for a football field than an office.

Wavy blond hair framed an extremely attractive face with its square jaw, long straight nose, and surprisingly full lips. Lila thought he looked a little too perfect. Too bad for all his looks, he harbored a black heart.

Though she'd read this article a dozen times, she continued on, looking for some kind of clue that might help her. Lila placed the newspaper on the coffee table and picked up a more recent issue. This particular article focused solely on the man and the accident which had nearly cost him his life. Obviously the accident didn't prevent him from ruining her father's life. Lila was tired of this waiting game. She had to act now.

It was time to confront The Beast.

Chapter Two

"I'm sorry, Hunter, but I can't do this anymore." Jessica delivered the statement with a voice full of contrition, but it still sounded artificial to Hunter's ears. Who did she think she was kidding?

"Do what?" he spoke with quiet menace. If she thought he'd let her off so easy then she had another think coming. He'd been down this road before and refused to be lied to. If Jessica wanted to end their affair, she'd have to be woman enough to be honest about her reasons.

She licked her glossy lips, a move that had once turned him on, but now simply annoyed him. "You know perfectly well what I mean. It's over between us. This relationship."

He lifted a brow. "What relationship? This is merely an arrangement, one for which you are not holding up your end of the bargain. You provide companionship when needed and give me pussy when and wherever I want it, in exchange all of your financial needs will be taken care of."

Jessica turned her nose up as if her delicate sensitivities had been offended. "Must you be so vulgar? You make me sound no better than a common street walker."

Hunter let out a humorless chuckle. "Cut the bullshit, Jessica. At least a common street walker as you put it is honest about what she does. Just because you have expensive tastes doesn't mean you should be placed on some kind of hooker hierarchy."

"I am not a prostitute. Why do you always have to be so difficult? This is exactly why I can't deal with you anymore."

14

"Because I won't stroke ego? Or because I tell it like it is. Answer this for me, if you're not exactly what I say you are, then why is it after every time we fuck, you mention a piece of jewelry or designer purse you need money for? Now, I don't mind giving it to you because as I've already stated, that was the arrangement and you're a decent fuck, but it seems a little mendacious of you to say you're no prostitute when you seek some type of compensation right after sex. I'm guessing you feel that it's nothing less than you deserve for having to put with this ugly mug of mine. I get it. But do me the favor of not insulting my intelligent."

"I..." She couldn't even finish whatever it was she wanted to say as she kept her eyed downcast.

Hunter shrugged in no mood to spare her feelings. "There's no need for you to go into any long explanation. I figured it was only a matter of time before you decided to end things between us. Maybe you've found another benefactor. Your type always does. Perhaps he's someone you can actually stand to look at without shuddering with revulsion."

"You're making me out to be the bad guy here and that's not fair."

"Life's not fucking fair, Jessica. You don't think I notice the way you cringe when my hair isn't completely covering my face? In the last few weeks, when I wanted you, you had a convenient excuse not to come but yet you still wanted your bills to get paid on time. You knew exactly what you were getting into when you got involved with me. Did you think you could just spend my money without delivering the goods? You aren't that beautiful."

Her mouth gaped open. "It wasn't like that," she protested, although she couldn't look him in the eyes when she said it.

"Then tell me what it was like. Tell me why you've reneged on this deal when you seemed so eager in the beginning." Hunter tried to keep the bitterness from seeping into his voice, but as he thought of how she'd double-crossed

15

him, he found the task more difficult with each passing moment. He knew exactly why she wanted out, but he wanted to hear the words from her mouth.

"I—I can't say."

"Say it, Goddamn you!" Hunter slammed his fist on the big oak desk separating them. If it wasn't in the way, he was sure his fingers would be wrapped around her lovely alabaster throat.

She jumped, fear entering her eyes for the first time since she'd entered his office. Good. It was better than pity or disgust. He should have known this would happen when Jessica decided to visit him at his office instead of coming to his home as she normally did. More witnesses. He'd known it was a matter of time before she left him like the others, but it didn't ease the pain searing within his chest. Did he have the right to be this angry or should he be grateful for the time she had given him? After all, who would want to stay with a disfigured freak like him? Still, a deal was a deal.

"Hunter, please don't make this more difficult for me than it already is."

"Why should I make this easy for you? Do you think things have been a piece of cake for me? Look at my face!"

She shook her head, dark red hair swirling around her face. "Don't make me. I can't...I can't handle it. I thought I could but the money isn't worth it. I—" She broke off with a sob. There were a number of hurtful things she could have said, but this by far was the worst.

"Just go," he whispered, not bothering to hide his disgust in himself or with her. He should have been used to this by now, but it hurt as bad as it did the first time. Lowering his head, Hunter waited for her to leave. When he didn't hear the sound of retreating feet, he roared, "What the hell are you still standing there for?"

A squeak escaped her lips as she nervously tucked a lock of auburn hair behind her ear. "But you said you'd take care of my bills this month."

The greedy little bitch. It would have served her right if he told her where to go, but the faster she was out of his life, the better.

"Forward them to my personal assistant and they'll be taken care of."

"Thank you." Jessica smiled, moving closer to his desk as if to shake his hand, but Hunter narrowed his eyes, not bothering to hide the rage building within him. She stopped in her tracks and nodded. "Uh, thank you. I'm sorry things didn't work out for us."

"Fuck off!"

Wisely she didn't respond.

When the door clicked shut, Hunter released a frustrated growl. With a sweep of his arm, he knocked everything off his desk, computer monitor and all. The items went crashing to the ground with a loud clatter.

Seconds later, the executive vice president, his second in command, opened his door and stuck his head in the office. "What the hell happened here?" Thomas inquired as he surveyed the mess Hunter had made.

No one in the Ramsey's organization dared talk to Hunter this way or question him, except Thomas. His years of service and friendship had given him that right. Thomas was also the only one who still looked Hunter directly in the face without flinching.

"What does it look like happened?" Hunter sneered, not wanting to discuss the loss of yet another lover.

"It looks like an adult has thrown a childish temper tantrum. I passed by your latest paramour in the hallway. I take it by the clutter you've made, you two are finished?"

"Nice guess work, Sherlock. What are you going to tell me next? That it's Tuesday?"

"If you ask me, you're better off without her. And you should have known better before getting involved with her in the first place. The only thing she was interested in was your wallet."

Sometimes Hunter wished Thomas wasn't so open with his thoughts. His situation was humiliating enough as it was with the reminder. "But I didn't ask you, so keep your damn opinions to yourself."

"Someone needs to open your eyes to a few home truths."

Hunter exhaled slowly, wishing his friend would just go away. "And I suppose you've appointed yourself to the task?"

"I'm only saying this because I care."

Hunter didn't need this bullshit. Not now. He turned his swivel chair around to face the window. "Don't you think I know what Jessica was after? Maybe that's why I chose her in the first place. At least that way there'd be no pretense of an emotion that doesn't exist."

Thomas released a sigh. "Why do you even bother with these women in the first place? You may get a temporary bedmate, but is it really satisfying if you have to pay for them? Jessica was little better than a prostitute."

Despite having said exactly that to Jessica a few minutes, early, Hunter didn't want to concede the point to his friend. He was humiliated enough as it was. "I believe the term is called mistress."

"Whatever you want to call it, you basically had to pay for her time. You can do better than that, Hunter."

Hunter turned around then to face Thomas. "And what would you have me do? Stroll into a party and chat up some random woman as if I don't look like a monster?"

Thomas rolled his eyes heavenward. "You're not a monster, and if you allowed someone to take the time to get to know you, then maybe you'd realize that too."

"Considering you have no clue what I'm going through, it's easy for you to say."

Thomas raked his fingers through his dark hair. "Look, if you're going to have another pity party then you're going to be the only guest."

"Then fucking leave! I didn't ask you to come in here to begin with!"

Thomas advanced, stopping when he stood directly in front of the desk. "I should, but someone has to deal with your disgruntled ass. Hunter, I can't pretend to know what it's like to go through what you have, but it can't be healthy to cut yourself off from the rest of the world. You stay holed up in that damned house of yours for days at a time, only coming to the office occasionally. And when you do show up here, you make such a big production of slipping in like a damn thief in the night because, heaven forbid, someone might catch a glimpse of the face you keep covered with hair. Did you ever think people are only reacting to what you project?"

"I don't—"

Thomas held up his hand. "Let me finish. You've had your say so I'm going to have mine. You refuse to meet with our business associates and it makes people wonder about your competency to run Ramsey's."

"That's what conference calls are for."

"And you know very well that doesn't always fly for our international clients."

"That's what you're here for. Do you have any complaints about how I conduct business?"

"That wasn't my point and you know it. Do you know what your problem is?"

Hunter's fingers curled into fists as he struggled to hold on to his threadbare temper. "No, but I'm sure you'll enlighten me."

"You're being an ass. Don't you realize how lucky you are to be alive? You might have a few scars, but at least you still have your life."

This had to be the hundredth time Thomas had delivered this speech and it was just as annoying this time around. "Saying it's a few scars is an understatement. And maybe I would have been better off dead, at least then I wouldn't have to go through life looking like a circus sideshow attraction."

Thomas shook his head. "You sound incredibly ridiculous right now. Get over yourself. It's time to come out of hiding."

Hunter pulled back his hair and stared defiantly at his friend. "Care to take another look and revise your expert opinion?" His scars were the very reason he refused to look in any mirrors and why he avoided them like the plague. God's little joke on him had been to leave one side of his face intact while the other side was a hideous roadmap of imperfections. The doctors had offered skin grafting, but had informed him that while some of the damage could be corrected, he would still never be the same as he was before.

There was a time when Hunter had been considered handsome. In fact, he used to revel in the attention he'd get from the opposite sex. Women and sometimes men would throw themselves at him. He'd even been featured in a local paper as one of New York's sexiest bachelors. He'd taken his looks for granted, but the accident changed everything. Now, he couldn't walk down the street without making small children cry. The humiliation of dealing with people's reactions made him isolate himself and withdraw from the social whirl he'd once enjoyed.

The most humbling aspect of life after the accident was the loneliness. Though he was at the top of his field he worked hard, but there was a time when he had partied just as hard. He spent long hours in the office, but on the weekends, he'd

20

been known for his wild parties. He'd been a regular feature in the society pages and usually he was photographed with a beautiful women, each more gorgeous than the next.

Hunter hadn't entertained since the accident and most of the staff that kept the mansion running properly had abandoned him as well. If he had a choice, he'd remained holed up in his house and never leave so that he wouldn't have to face people's stares. The flat out rejection of society wasn't the worst, however. It was the pitying stares that got to him the most. Where people once stared at him because he was good-looking, now they looked because he was hideous. Were it not for Thomas forcing him to handle his responsibility to Ramsey's, Hunter would probably never bother leaving his home. Even the women he'd set up as mistresses couldn't stomach him for long, as demonstrated by Jessica.

He shouldn't bother, but goddammit, he was still a man with needs. Masturbation would only satisfy him to a point, but what choice did he have other than choosing some random woman off the street. The very thought disgusted him. At least when he had a steady lover, they were exclusive with him and he'd always verified their clean bills of health before entering into an agreement. Perhaps it was a part of his life he'd have to let go. He wasn't sure if he could deal with the constant rejection, because it was slowly killing him on the inside.

Some would probably say he was getting exactly what he deserved. Remembering what an ex-lover had told him a few years back, he closed his eyes.

He'd just ended their affair with his customary parting gift of diamond earrings and a matching tennis bracelet. "You're a bastard, Hunter Jamison, and one day you're going to get your comeuppance. You're going to fall for a woman who won't love you back, and by God, I wish I could be there to see it!" his ex had cried.

Hunter, in his cocky insolence, had laughed in her face before dismissing her from his thoughts. He'd found her words amusing though. What did he need with love? He had wealth, power, and access to unlimited pussy. Love was for losers. Hadn't he learned that particular lesson well enough from his mother who went through husbands like most people did underwear and his father who spent years pining for a woman who didn't care for anyone but herself?

Hunter had yet to find a woman worthy of the emotion *if* it even existed. Still, it didn't mean he wanted to go without companionship. Who would?

Thomas finally threw his arms up in the air in his exasperation. "I wish you'd get over yourself, Hunter. Yes, you're scarred, but you still have your health and your life. You have a successful business and several possessions most people would kill for. How about being thankful for the things you do have?"

"Because those things don't mean a thing as long as I look like this." Hunter pointed to his face.

Thomas shook his head, annoyance etched on every line of his round face. "I give up. Have it your way. You're a disfigured monstrosity who no one will ever love. There. Is that what you'd rather hear?"

Hunter shrugged. "It's the truth."

Thomas sighed with obvious frustration. "I hope you really don't believe that."

"I do."

"Then I feel sorry for you."

"I didn't ask for your goddamn pity, nor do I want it."

"Fine. I'll leave you to your misery."

Hunter knew Thomas meant well but it was easy for someone with a normal face to spout that bullshit about having a lot to live for. But still, maybe he was a bit more harsh than necessary. Regardless of the fact they didn't see eye to eye on this particular subject, he didn't want his friend to leave on this note. "Wait. Don't leave. You obviously had a reason for coming to my office in the first place. What's up?"

Thomas looked like he was heavily debating staying or going, but finally took a seat across from Hunter's desk.

"We're still having problems with the last owner on Hudson Street. He refuses to sell. According to the attorneys, he's had some health problems of late and his daughter is making most of the decisions for him."

"Does she have power of attorney?"

"Legally, I'm not certain, but it seems Mr. Saunders seems to be okay with her speaking for him."

This was the one project that Hunter still had interest in. It had been his baby from the beginning. "She's probably holding out for more money. If that's the case then she's in for a rude awaking. We offered her a fair market price given the condition of the area. That little building doesn't have much worth now that everyone else has sold."

"Exactly," Thomas agreed. "Seeing as most of the tenants are relocating, she's aware that their little shop can't remain in business without any customers. But the problem is, even if they close the store, Saunders still owns the building outright and he occupies the apartment above it. He used to rent out the other units but those tenants have since moved. But from what I can tell, the mortgage has been paid off so we can't use that as leverage."

"We've dealt with difficult people in these situations before. I'm sure there's a way around this."

"There is. We've already initiated plan B. We have a couple council members who owe us some favors. I believe the property will be ours before the year is out, but we can at least start building around it."

"Good, I think—" Loud shouting on the other side of the door interrupted Hunter's train of thought, making him wonder what the hell was happening.

"You can't go in there! Oww! I'm calling the police!" That sounded like his usually unflappable personal assistant.

"Fine. Do what you have to do, and so will I," answered someone whose voice Hunter didn't recognize. A woman's voice.

Seconds later the door flew open, and standing in the doorway was one of the most beautiful women he'd ever seen.

And she looked pissed.

Chapter Three

The moment Lila stepped into her adversary's office, all the courage she'd summoned for this confrontation flew out the window. Staring at her with the greenest eyes she'd ever seen was the legend himself. Hunter Jamison.

Her feet wouldn't carry her forward, and she couldn't tear her gaze away from the man sitting behind the large oak desk in the corner of the office.

"Mr. Jamison, I tried to keep her out, but she assaulted me. I've called the police and security is on their way upstairs." The woman who'd tried to restrain her entered the office. She sounded out of breath. Probably from chasing Lila, who'd run past her.

Lila didn't set out to give the woman a hard time, someone who was after all just doing her job but she was determined to have this meeting come hell or high water. Turning around to face her accuser, Lila pasted a smile on her face, and delivered her next line in a saccharine sweet tone. "I didn't assault you. If I hurt you because I was forced to use a self-defense maneuver when you suddenly grabbed me then the blame falls at your feet. You're the one who initiated physical contact. Maybe when the police get here, I should file assault charges on you."

The woman gasped, her mouth opening and then shutting as if she couldn't believe what she was hearing. "B-but you're trespassing. No one would believe you."

"Well, I guess we'll let the police decide when they get here." Lila twirled back around and noticed a stocky dark-haired man with glasses standing by the boss man. Had he been there already? He must have, but Lila only had eyes for Mr. Jamison at first. Among other things she'd missed when she entered the room, papers and other office supplies scattered the floor along with a computer monitor. This place looked as a tornado had been through it.

Refocusing her attention on the still figure behind the desk, she noticed a thick mane of wavy blond hair resting in a cascade around his shoulders, obscuring most of his face. The only features she could really make out were those arresting eyes, a long blade of a nose, and sensuously full lips, which were now pulled down into a ferocious frown.

"Miss, whoever the hell you are, you're going to have to leave," the dark-haired man spoke.

Lila spared him a brief glance, before returning her attention to her target. "I'm not going anywhere until *he* agrees to cease and desist!" She jerked her thumb in Jamison's direction and advanced toward the desk. "Don't you understand what you're doing? Do you get your kicks from destroying people's lives?"

The unknown man walked toward her, but she backed away when it looked as if he'd grab her. "If you touch me, I'm going to kick you in the balls."

That warning seemed to be enough to make him stand down. He held his hands up defensively. "Ma'am, I'm not sure what the problem is, but perhaps if you come to my office, we can work something out to your satisfaction. My name is Thomas Ruby and I'm just as capable to see to your problem as anyone in this organization."

It was a tactic to get her to leave if she'd ever heard one. Lila wasn't stupid. He'd have her ass hauled out the building the minute she stepped out of this room.

"No! The only person I want to talk to is Hunter Jamison, and if that's not your name, we have nothing to discuss."

Why wasn't the big blond saying anything? His head was bowed now, but she sensed his anger simmering just below the surface. Good. That made two of them.

"Look, Miss..." Mr. Ruby trailed off in an attempt to get her name.

"Saunders. Lila Saunders," she bit out through gritted teeth.

Mr. Ruby stepped away from her, mouth agape. "Miss Saunders, I—" His words were cut off when two uniformed security guards burst into the office and ran over to her.

Each of them grabbed one of her arms. Lila refused to let this crusade end at the hands of a couple of rent-a-cops. "Let go of me!" She wiggled and struggled against their grasps, trying to pull free even though the more she moved, the tighter their hold became. They were too strong for her. *Please don't let it end this way,* she silently prayed.

"The police are on their way, sir," a pimple-faced guard said as his nails dug into her skin. "We'll keep her downstairs until they arrive. We're not sure how she got up here, but it won't happen again."

Lila continued to fight, trying to yank free. "Get off of me!"

"Let her go." The deep booming voice that resonated throughout the entire office came from the man himself, shocking her so much she froze.

"But, Mr. Jamison, we—"

"Let her go. I'll deal with this matter myself." Hunter Jamison pushed away from his desk and stood up to reveal his magnificent height. He had to be at least six feet six and he was very broad.

"But the police are on the way!" the woman whined.

"Then tell them you've wasted their time. I'll talk to Miss Saunders."

"But—" The woman didn't seem ready to give in so easily.

"This discussion isn't up for debate, Anita," Mr. Jamison said the words softly enough, but the underlying message was there: do as I say or else.

The security guards released Lila's arms with obvious reluctance. She rubbed her aching limbs to increase the blood flow to the areas they'd squeezed as she shot each guard a glare.

"Thomas, please leave us," Jamison ordered.

Mr. Ruby remained where he stood for a moment, but one look from the boss had his shoulders sagging in defeat. "Fine, but if you need me, I'll be in my office." He gave Lila a shaky smile before following the other three out. He closed the door behind him with a decisive click.

Once she and Mr. Jamison were alone, Lila squared her shoulders and took a deep breath. His large frame would have intimidated anyone, but she refused to be cowed by him. She raised her chin in a gesture of defiance and met his gaze.

"Miss Saunders, please have a seat," he offered. The way he stared at her made Lila feel self-conscious. She couldn't quite read his expression, especially with all that hair in his face, but she felt like a very juicy mouse beneath the hungry gaze of a cat.

Placing her hands on her hips, she shook her head. "No, thank you. I'd prefer to stand. What I have to say won't take long."

He shrugged one massive shoulder. "Suit yourself. I'll sit, if you don't mind."

The office was huge, but he seemed to dominate every square inch of it, though she did wonder about the mess. Lila didn't like the way she was so aware of his larger than life presence. She licked her suddenly dry lips. "N-no I don't mind."

"Good, Miss… May I call you Lila?"

"Yes."

"Lila," he said her name slowly, as though testing it on his tongue. "Did you know your name means dark-haired beauty? I took a little Arabic in college."

She did, actually. Her father had mentioned it to her once, and how it was the only name he and her mother had agreed on. "I didn't come here to talk about the meaning of my name."

He inclined his head slightly forward, making his hair cover up even more of his face. Was he really as badly scarred as the newspapers suggested? "Fair enough. Then tell me why you've come to see 'the Beast'"

Lila knew he was toying with her, but she didn't come here to play games. She'd be damned if she let him frighten her. "I'm sure you already know."

"You're the one who burst into my office. If you have the guts to do that, I'm certain you can follow through by sharing your grievance."

Bastard. Did he want her to beg? On the verge of telling him to go to hell, she remembered how sick and weak her father had seemed this morning. If Hunter Jamison wanted his pound of flesh, she'd give it to him. She would do whatever it took to save Saunders.

"I'm asking you to reconsider your offer on my father's property."

"Our plans have been finalized. The shopping center will go up as planned."

"But you can build around Saunders, can't you? I've seen the blueprints. My father's building will be just on the outskirts of it."

"The shopping complex could use the space for parking," he countered. "Anyway, it's in your best interest to sell out, don't you think? Wouldn't your father's little business suffer from the competition?"

Lila gritted her teeth at his condescending tone. Her fingers itched to slap him. "We'll make it work somehow."

His lips tilted into a small brief smile. "You sound like you actually believe that, but I'm afraid you're wasting your time. I'm sure you're already aware the city council has taken an interest in your father's property. Once they're involved, there's little I can do about it."

Lila bit back the expletive hovering on her tongue, silently counting to ten before speaking. "If you wanted to, you could."

He grinned. "You're right. I could, but I don't feel so inclined.

. "What you're doing is illegal."

"Funny thing about the law. If you can afford to hire the best attorneys, they always find a way to work around it."

Her chest felt tight as Lila felt herself losing a handle of the situation. "Then I'll hire my own lawyer and fight you every step of the way. I'll make sure your plans are thwarted and tie you up in court for years."

A smirk twisted his lips, mocking her. "A lawyer? I have several at my disposal at the top of their field. How long do you think you can last against them?"

"As long as it take."

"The last I checked attorneys don't work for free. Do you have the disposable income to see a case like this through when in the end, you'll lose anyway?"

Lila clenched her hands at her sides wanting to smack that taunting grin from his face but she couldn't afford to antagonize him, at least not yet. "You've already destroyed my childhood. Most of the businesses that I loved so much growing up have already gone. You've left the neighborhood a virtual ghost town. And now you not only want to effectively shut down my father's shop, you want to kick us out of our home." By telling him this, she hoped that it would appeal to any bit of humanity he had within him.

Again, he shrugged. "Tell that to someone who's interested, sweetheart."

Lila wasn't prepared to let things end like this. There had to be something she could do. As much as she loathed to do so, she was willing to beg. "Please, Mr. Jamison, there must be some other way. I'm pleading with you. Don't do this. If my father loses his business, it would kill him."

"Don't you think you're being a tad dramatic, Lila?"

She began to shake as she willed herself to remain where she stood. "I'm telling the truth. Saunders is his life. The stress of your company's constant harassment has taken a toll on his health."

Jamison stifled a yawn, not looking the least bit impressed. "If keeping his business is so important, why isn't your father here pleading his own case? What kind of man would allow his daughter to fight his battles for him? This doesn't sound like the kind of person I'd do a favor for."

Lila realized he was trying to bait her, but she wouldn't let him. No matter how much she wanted to tell the smug son of a bitch where to go, she'd have to keep her cool.

"My father doesn't know I'm here. He's...he hasn't been well lately, but the only thing that makes him better is working at the store. He lives for that place. If you take it away from him, he'd have nothing to live for."

"Do you mean you're not reason enough for him to live?"

"You're twisting my words around. That isn't what I meant at all. To be honest, he plans on giving up and just taking the money."

Jamison's brows knitted, his bewilderment evident. "Then why are you here?"

"Because I know he doesn't want to. He's doing it for me. He thinks if he sells, I can move on with my life. My father believes he's a burden to me."

"Perhaps there's some wisdom in his decision. You're young, beautiful...and desirable. Why would you want to throw your life away taking care of an old man?"

Lila tightened her fists. *I will stay calm. I will stay calm*, she chanted in her mind. "My father could never be a burden to me because I love him very much, but then again, I wouldn't expect a cold bastard like you to understand."

Jamison leaned back in his chair, raising a dark blond brow. "Strong words for someone who wants my help."

Lila turned her head unable to meet his taunting green gaze. "I'm sorry, I shouldn't have said it."

"Don't be. It's what you meant. I can respect that."

She forced herself to look at him again. "Look, Mr. Jamison, I know if you'll just let us be, he'll get better and won't worry so much. Due to pressure your company is placing on him, I fear this stress is taking a toll on his health."

His lips twitched into a mockery of a smile. "Beautiful and compassionate. A rare combination. You're to be commended on your concern for your father, but you've made a miscalculation."

"What do you mean?" she whispered, almost afraid to hear the answer.

"You bet all your hopes on the fact I'd give a damn. Unfortunately for you, I don't."

Lila's breath caught in her throat as she blinked hard. She vowed not to cry in front of this jerk. It took several moments before she could compose herself enough to reply. "I'll do anything if you would reconsider."

He stiffened and his eyes narrowed. "Anything?"

Lila closed her eyes tightly to block the sight of his hateful presence. Did those words actually leave her mouth? "Anything."

"I'm not sure you know what you're saying. When you make a provocative statement like that, you're asking for trouble." His gaze blatantly roamed her body, leaving no doubt in her mind what he was thinking. "Now tell me, Lila, are you willing to back up that statement? Because I have no time for little girls playing adult games."

Was she really propositioning him? Her father had taught her to have respect for herself and her body, yet here she was offering to act the whore for someone she despised more than anything. Could she go through with this? She moistened her lips with the tip of her tongue nervously. Not trusting herself to speak, she nodded.

"Would you sleep with me?" he asked softly.

Even though she'd known this was the direction the conversation was headed when she'd made her bold declaration, his words still came as a shock. To actually hear them said aloud made her feel sleazy, but now that it was all on the table, there was no turning back.

Lila felt like a character in a bad B movie. Did things like this really happen? Her stomach twisted in knots and her hands shook. If she pinched herself, would she wake up from the horrible nightmare? "I was actually hoping you had some ounce of decency inside of you but apparently I was mistaken."

"It's a simple yes or no question, Miss Saunders. You said you'd do anything to save your father's property and I'm simply putting that claim to the test."

"But why me? We don't know each other."

"Does one need to know their partner in order to fuck?"

She flinched at the crudeness of his statement. "You're disgusting."

33

"What I am is honest. And to answer your previous question, why not you? You're certainly beautiful, but I'm sure you're well aware of that. Women like you usually are. And let's just say, I admire your spirit. So what do you say Miss Saunders? Are you willing to go above and beyond for your father? You have approximately three seconds to give me your answer before I remove the offer from the table and call the guards again to escort you out."

What choice did she have? "Yes," she finally answered after nearly losing her nerve.

His expression didn't change and he didn't respond immediately. It was almost as if her answer didn't matter to him one way or the other and he was just trying to push Lila to violence.

"Well?" she demanded some kind of reaction from him.

He leaned back in his chair and folded his hands together. "What I want is a mistress. I find myself without one at the moment, and I think you'll do quite nicely. Would you be willing to stay with me for three months at my house, at my beck and call — seeing to my every need?"

"You only mentioned one time. I thought —"

"No, I asked if you were willing to sleep with me. I never gave you the terms. For those three months, I indeed to have you as many times as I please."

She should have been disgusted but founded herself mesmerized by that green gaze. Something had to be seriously wrong with her that she found this man anything other than reprehensible. Still, what choice did she have? "But my father —"

"Would be taken care of."

"I don't want to be away from him for that long."

"Then you obviously don't care as much about saving his business as you've let on. Good day, Miss Saunders."

34

The tears that had threatened to spill earlier sprang to her eyes once again. "Wait! The answer is yes, but only if you arrange for a nurse to stop by every day to see my dad takes his medication and for someone to help him around the store."

"While it's pretty bold of you to make demands considering you're the one who wants a favor of me, that can easily be arranged."

She let her head fall, as shame washed over her. What had she done? "Okay, then it's a deal."

"And would you be ready for me to fuck you whenever and however I want?"

She winced. "You don't have to be so crude about it."

"Sweetheart, I don't have time to tiptoe around your ladylike sensibilities. Besides, I won't insult either of us by calling it making love."

"It could never be that," she hissed.

"As I've already said, I like your spirit, Lila." He stood up and then stalked over to her.

She took a step back. "Hold on. How do I know you'll honor your end of the bargain and leave my father's business alone?"

"I'll have my attorney draft a contract and make it legal and binding. There will be no mention of sex in the actually document for legal reasons but when you see the term 'companion' then you'll know exactly what that means. At the end of our agreement, you'll receive a generous settlement in addition to services rendered."

Lila shook her head. "I don't want your money, just your promise to leave my father be."

Jamison raised a brow. "Persistent, aren't you? But before we reach a formal agreement, I think there's something you should see…in case you want to change your mind."

"I won't."

35

"We'll see." Slowly he raised his hands to his face and pulled his hair back, revealing what it had been hiding. On one side of his face was an angry jumble of deep, red scars running from his temple to his neck. They created such a contrast to the other side of his face which was virtually untouched, she gasped in horror. She'd heard that he was a recluse because of a near-fatal accident and now she understood why. He was clearly ashamed of his disfigurement. As a nurse, she'd seen much worse, but they took her by surprise nonetheless. Mainly, her shock had stemmed the fact that she hadn't been expecting it. She

She hadn't eaten since lunch the night before because she'd been too nervous about her upcoming confrontation with Hunter Ramsey. It seemed like it had finally caught up to her because she suddenly felt dizzy and the room began to spin, and everything went black. Her last conscious memory was the sensation of falling.

What the hell had he been thinking to throw that impulsive offer at Lila Saunders? Had he become that desperate? One thing he knew for certain, she was one of, if not *the* most stunning woman he'd laid eyes on.

Tall and voluptuous with curves that cried out to be caressed, she had the face of an angel. Hunter had memorized her every feature, from her rich dark brown skin that looked as soft as spun silk, full bow-shaped lips and tilt-tipped nose. Her hair had been pulled back in a crown of glorious curls, emphasizing high cheek bones. He wondered how her dark tresses would look flowing around her shoulders, or arranged around her head against a pillow — in his bed.

His cock grew hard at the mere thought. Lila's most arresting feature he'd determined, were a pair of large dark gold eyes framed by long thick lashes. She was a real beauty.

Hunter took another swig of his scotch as he remembered the look of horror on her face when he'd revealed his scars. As he'd suspected, Lila was just like the others. She'd talked a good game, but she didn't have the nerve to back it up. Despite this being a business transaction, he should have known a woman who looked like her couldn't possibly be attracted to him. In most cases, he would have brushed off her reaction and written her off, but for some reason, he couldn't.

He should have sent Lila on her way the second she'd come to, but in the moment he'd caught her from falling, holding her in his arms, Hunter had realized it was something he wanted to experience over and over again. But still, his pride wouldn't allow him to demand she follow through with her offer. Instead, he'd handed her his card and informed her she had twenty-four hours to contact him before the offer was taken off the table.

He wouldn't hear from her, he was sure.

She may have been able to give her delectable body to him if he kept the scars hidden, but as long as they were out in the open, she couldn't handle it. It figured. Lila had made some excuse about passing out from lack of food but he was certain she was lying. Her reaction was no different from the countless women who had the misfortune to see his face. Even his assistant Ann, could barely bring herself to look him in the eyes.

Hunter couldn't remember the last time he'd wanted someone with the intensity that he felt for Lila, but he knew he'd have to get over it fast and get used to living a life of solitude. Maybe when the shopping center project was over, he'd resign from the company and sell his stocks. Going out in public was becoming more difficult each time.

"Mr. Jamison, you have a phone call," his housekeeper, Mrs. Coates interrupted his thoughts.

He hadn't heard it ring, not that it mattered. It was probably Thomas. "Tell Thomas I'll call him later."

"It's not Mr. Ruby. It's a Miss Saunders. Would you like to speak to her or should I tell her you're unavailable?"

Lila? Was this a courtesy call to tell him she had changed her mind? He set the decanter and his glass aside. "I'll take it in here. Thank you."

Mrs. Coates nodded and left the room. Hunter picked up the receiver and waited for his housekeeper to hang up the other line before speaking. "Lila. To what do I owe the pleasure of your call?" He silently congratulated himself for sounding calm.

"You know." She spoke in a hushed whisper as if someone was there with her.

"So what's your answer?"

She took so long to reply, he thought the line had disconnected.

"Hello?"

A sigh greeted his ears. "Yes. My answer is yes—that is, if you still want me."

She had no idea how much.

Chapter Four

It looked like Hunter had thought of everything, from hiring a private nurse for her father to ensuring the store would be taken care of properly in her absence. Lila had even taken a physical and STD tests at his insistence, verifying her clean bill of health. Lila had been on the pill since she was a teenager to regulate her cycle, but it had been humiliating to be asked whether she was on some type of birth control. As a show of good faith, he'd presented her his medical records to prove his vitality and disease-free status.

Hunter had told Lila he wanted her without any barriers between them.

She had to be crazy to go through with this. To actually be this man's kept woman for the next few months was something that had kept her awake at night since she'd said yes. He'd wanted her to come as she was, with the clothes on her back he'd said, and nothing more other than what was necessary as everything else would be provided for her.

He'd even sent a car to pick her up and take her to his home. The hardest part in preparing to spend this time with him was coming up with an excuse to give her father for being away. Lila hated lying to him. He'd been so trusting when she told him she'd been offered a private nursing assignment.

In fact, her story seemed to make him happy, to see her venture out "and not be closed in with the old man" as he'd put it. Lila hadn't been able to look him in the eye. How could one tell their dad they were going to whore themselves out—after all, what she was doing was little better than prostitution.

Shivering as a pair of brilliant green eyes flashed through her mind, she was tempted to tell the driver to turn the car around and take her home. The words hovered on the tip of her tongue, but they wouldn't come out. For the past few weeks, the amount of time Hunter had given her to change her mind, she'd fought desperately to come to terms with what she'd agreed to.

She'd have to let him touch and screw her in ways she'd let no other man do to her before. She was no virgin, but the few lovers she'd had, Lila had given herself to, she'd been in established relationships with. The odd thing was, the thought of being with Hunter Ramsey didn't make her cringe as she felt it should have. What was wrong with her? Did she look forward to being debased by him?

"Ma'am, we're here."

The cool burst of air hitting her skin signaled to Lila the rear passenger door was open. She'd been so lost in her musings, she hadn't realized the car had stopped. The sudden urge to get out and run and keep running grabbed her momentarily. Once she entered Hunter Jamison's home, there would be no turning back. Could she go through with this?

Clenching her fists at her sides, she closed her eyes and squeezed them tight, attempting to work up enough nerve to get out of the car.

"Ma'am, we're here," the driver repeated.

Lila nodded, opening her eyes. It wasn't just a nightmare. Damn. "Okay. Thank you." Taking a deep breath, she took the hand offered her. For the first time since the car had stopped she looked at surroundings. So this was where she'd be staying? To say the house—no the mansion—was large would have been an understatement. Lila had only seen something of its kind on those television shows which gave peeks into the opulent lives of celebrities. The large beige Georgian style manor with its imposing columns could have been considered a work of art in its beauty.

The estate gave her another reason to hate Hunter Jamison. Here he lived high on the hog while harassing working class people like her father and forcing them out of their livelihoods.

Squaring her shoulders, she allowed the driver to lead her up the pathway to a side entrance. When they entered, Lila couldn't help but be awed by the grandness. She made a mental note not to touch anything while she was here because any of the treasures decorating this place would be far too dear for her to replace.

A tall, slender woman with warm, sherry-colored eyes and iron gray hair approached, a half smile on her lips. "Welcome, Miss Saunders. I'm Maddie Coates. I take care of this house for Mr. Jamison and during your stay here, I'll see to your needs. My husband, Ernest, drove you here. He'll also be on hand if I'm not available. There's an intercom in every room so you'll be able to contact us at any time."

Lila shook her head, nervous laughter trilling from her throat. "I won't bother you at all hours of the night. And please, call me Lila. You don't have to be so formal with me."

"If that's your wish…Miss Lila. Please follow me." The woman seemed nice enough, but Lila could tell she was a stickler for propriety. Sheesh, Lila hadn't realized people like Mrs. Coates existed outside of television and books. She and her husband were faithful retainers to the core. But then again, none of what was happening to her seemed real.

Already, Lila felt grossly out of place in a pair of slacks and a blouse she'd always believed she looked nice in. But her surroundings were a jarring reminder that her clothes had come off the rack and not in one of those fancy boutiques where someone who was used to this set up shopped. Her jaw dropped when she saw the room she'd be staying in. It was larger than all the rooms combined in the apartment she shared with her father.

41

"I hope this room is to your satisfaction, Miss Lila."

She could only nod in response. The room would have been adequate for the Queen of England. "Yes...it's very nice."

"Your private bathroom is through that door." Mrs. Coates pointed to a door at the far corner of the room. Then she walked to another section and opened a set of double doors. "Through the door on your right is your private sitting room. This is your closet. You'll find all your clothing in here and the dresser drawers. I'll leave you to freshen up and change into something for dinner, which will be served in a half hour. Mr. Jamison will be waiting for you in the dining room. Is there anything you require in the meantime?"

Lila was still trying to acclimate herself to the sheer luxury around her. "No, thank you."

Mrs. Coates hesitated at the door. "Mr. Jamison would like for you to choose something suitable to wear. He said you'd you know what he meant." The distaste in the other woman's tone brought heat to Lila's cheeks.

It was one thing to deal with her shame privately, but to have someone judging her put things in a whole different ball court. "Umm, yes," she murmured, not meeting the other woman's eyes.

Once the door clicked shut behind the housekeeper, Lila was able to let her guard down. She released the breath she didn't realized she'd been holding and headed to the closet. As gasp rushed from her lips when she stepped inside to see all the clothing surrounding her. There were gowns, blouses, shoes, hats and all kinds of accessories. It seem that Hunter's assistant had thought of everything. Ann Weathersby had contacted her to find out her sizes on Hunter's behalf. Lila had figured she'd have a few items to get her through the month, but she hadn't expected a complete wardrobe. She could probably wear a different outfit every day for the next three months and still not run out of clothing. The drawers were filled with fancy underwear and lingerie.

As she glanced at a label on one of the dresses Lila noticed it was a designer label. All of these items were probably from some ridiculous expensive line that she wouldn't have been able to afford on her budget. It probably didn't put a dent in his Hunter's budget while the other people worked hard to make enough to pay the bills. For the thousandth time, Lila wondered if she'd actually be able to get through the entire three months without backing out of the deal. What was she getting herself into to by agreeing to this crazy deal? Living in his home, and being fed and clothed by him? Would he be a selfish lover, demanding all she had, taking while giving nothing back? Yes, that's how it would be. A man who would steamroll over an entire neighborhood was probably not good in bed.

Not that it mattered. She'd just have to remain focused on her father's health. Hunter could be Don Juan for all she cared. Lila was determined to not enjoy it. She tried to stave off the tremble that moved up her spine. She'd made this bargain with the devil. Now, she'd have to figure out how not to get burned.

Hunter gripped the stem of his wine goblet, swirling the burgundy contents inside. What the hell was taking her so long? He knew the exact time she'd arrived—an hour ago. He'd left instructions with Mrs. Coates to escort Lila to the dining room a half hour after her arrival. He'd seen her get out of the car from his office window—saw how she'd looked at her surroundings with an air of uncertainty, touching something deep within him. Then he'd witnessed her lift that determined little chin of hers and stride into his house as proud as a queen.

Lila didn't strike him as the type to back down from a challenge, which made him wonder why she hadn't come downstairs to the dining room as he'd ordered. Had she lost her nerve? Hunter gritted his teeth, slamming the glass on the table, uncaring of the droplets of merlot splashing on the white lace tablecloth. He'd spent every single night since making this arrangement with her, lying awake, imagining his hands caressing her creamy chocolate body, her lush lips crushed beneath his. Then, he'd think about turning her over and riding that voluptuous rump and asking himself how she'd respond to toys. He tortured himself with questions of how things would be between them.

He supposed time would tell if only she would get her ass downstairs so he could lay down some ground rules. Glancing impatiently at the platinum Rolex adorning his wrist, Hunter decided he'd give her five more minutes before he stormed upstairs and dragged her down—by her hair, if he needed to.

The soft clicking of heels against the marble floor in the foyer alerted him to someone's approach. Lila.

Folding his hands in front of him, he tried to project an air of nonchalance he didn't feel. His pulse raced, and breath caught in his throat when she appeared.

Wearing a little black dress, which dipped in the front to reveal the top of her tempting cleavage and accentuated her curves to a tee, she stood proud and graceful. He could probably span her tiny waist with his hands. Lila wore her hair piled on top of her head and her face was bare of makeup save for a touch of gloss.

She was absolutely gorgeous. And late.

"You were supposed to be down here a half hour ago!" The words rushed from his mouth like an angry roar. It was a bit harsher than he'd intended. Hunter hadn't meant to let on how eager he'd been for her to join him.

Lila jumped at his brutal rejoinder before standing even straighter and taking a seat at the foot of the formal dining room table. "I'm here now." She replied so calmly, it raised his ire.

"You're too far away. Come down here."

Golden brown eyes narrowed as she raised her chin in defiance. "I prefer where I'm sitting, thank you."

There could only be one reason why she wouldn't want to be so close to him. Well, that was too damned bad. She'd have to accept him, scars and all. She'd already seen them and knew exactly what she was getting into. "Perhaps you've forgotten, but I call the shots around here. Not you. But seeing as how you'd like to test me, I'll give you two options, you can either take the seat here," he pointed to the table setting next to his, "or I'll come get you. I don't think you'd appreciate the experience."

Lila went completely still, her gaze locking with his. For a moment he believed she'd stand her ground, but in an abrupt movement, she pushed her chair back, and stood, her lips tightened to a thin, angry line.

Disappointment at her reluctance to be close nagged at him. One of the things that had struck him when she'd come downstairs was that Lila had seemed unaffected by his appearance. Oh, he'd seen that look of horror flash in her eyes upon the initial reveal in his office, and of course she'd fainted, but just now she'd almost seemed as if she'd forgotten about them. Could he have just imagined it? Was it simply wishful thinking on his part? Probably. He was a fool.

She was no different than anyone else. Too bad for her she'd have to deal with him for the next three months. Hunter had given up a great deal to give in to her demands, including hours with board members, executives, contractors and on top of that, coming up with a feasible alternative to his previous plans. He'd be damned if he allowed her to treat him like a fucking nuisance.

When she plopped down in the seat cattycorner to him, Lila lifted her shoulders in a shrug. "Okay. I'm here."

A floral scent wafted to his nostrils making Hunter want to bury his face against neck. Her proximity was doing things to his equilibrium he didn't think possible. His cock stirred and stiffened, straining against his pants. Goddamn. This woman had to be part witch because she'd cast a spell on him. There was only one way to grab control of the situation and that was to let her know right away who was in charge.

"Rule number one, when I say jump, you'll ask how high. Two, when I tell you to be somewhere at a designated time, I expect you to make it happen. Three, you will always be courteous to my staff. And last but not least, failure to obey my rules will result in punishment."

Her lips twisted into a smirk. "Punishment? What do you plan on doing? Giving me a time out?"

"You'll find out when you fail to do as I ask."

Mrs. Coates chose that moment to enter the dining room. "Mr. Jamison, are you ready for me to serve the meal?"

"Yes, thank you."

The housekeeper turned to Lila. "Would you like a glass of wine, Miss Lila?"

"Yes, she would."

With a nod Mrs. Coates left them alone once again.

Fire flashed from the depths of her golden eyes and if looks could kill, Hunter was sure he'd be dead on the spot. A smile tugged at the corners of her lips. He couldn't help admiring her spirit.

"I can speak for myself and I don't particularly care for wine at the moment."

"Do you have some objection to drinking alcohol?"

"I don't, but I'd rather not have any now."

"But I want you to have some. It would please me."

Her lips quirked. "And what you say goes right?"

"You're a fast learner." He allowed his gaze to drift to the tops of her breasts. Unable to go another second without touching her, Hunter reached over and ran his finger across her tantalizing décolletage.

Lila gasped, eyes widening. She jerked away from his hand. "Don't."

"It's my prerogative to touch you. Remember our bargain… How is your father by the way?"

"You're a beast," she mumbled under her breath.

A chuckle escaped his lips. "So they say. And you, my dear, are a beauty and you're mine—that is unless you've changed your mind?"

Through the narrowed slits of her eyes, Hunter thought he saw a suspicious gleam of moisture. He should have been ashamed for what he was in essence making her do, but he pushed that feeling away quickly. Lila was here of her own free will. It wasn't as if he were holding a gun to her head to make her stay. So she could save her tears for someone who gave a shit. "Has anyone ever told you how beautiful you are when you're angry? I'm happy to see the clothes the personal shopper selected for you fit so well."

Lila shrugged. "I don't see why I couldn't bring my own things."

"Because it suits me to see you dressed in satins and silks. My women wouldn't be caught in anything but the best. When our agreement is over, you may take them with you."

The chin was raised once again. "I'll walk away with what I came into this house with, if it's all the same to you."

He lifted his wine goblet and took a healthy sip before returning it to the table. "Suit yourself. They're yours to do with as you wish."

Mrs. Coates returned, wheeling a cart with their dinner on it.

Hunter leaned against the back of his chair, realizing Lila had barely looked at his face since she'd entered the dining room. Even those few times when she'd dared to catch his gaze, Lila had quickly looked away. The old insecurities hit him like a sledgehammer. *It doesn't matter what she thinks. She's yours for the taking.*

With slow deliberation, he pushed his hair away from his face. A perverse need for her to look at him as he was took over. "Look at me, Lila." He kept his voice low and soft, but left no room for doubt that he'd issued a command.

She raised her head with obvious reluctance and looked him square in eyes, gold fire sparking within the depths of her gaze. "Do you get off by telling me what to do?" She bit the words out, tight-lipped.

Hunter laughed. "Not from giving orders, but I plan on getting off in quite another way very soon."

Mrs. Coates placed his plate in front of him, her movements stiff. She was too much of a professional to give away her true thoughts, but Hunter had a feeling his housekeeper didn't approve of his arrangement. He'd brought women to the house before, but he'd never had one stay longer than a weekend. Not that it mattered what his employee thought anyway. This was his house, and he'd do what he saw fit in it.

Once he and Lila were alone again, he took another sip of his wine, watching as she pushed the food around her plate with her fork, not attempting to eat any of it.

"Do you have anything against your dinner?"

Her head came up again, bewilderment crinkling her forehead.

"You've been stabbing that steak with your fork as if it's done something to you. Is it too rare for your liking or do you not eat meat?"

She pushed her plate away. "I have no problem with eating meat. I'm not hungry."

"Try to eat something. You'll need your strength for later on."

Her eyes widened, her mouth forming a perfect, "o". "Look, Mr. Jamison—"

"Hunter. I hope you don't intend to go all formal on me every time I annoy you. Seeing as how we'll be getting to know each other." He paused to allow his gaze to rake over the length of her beckoning curves, quite intimately. "There's no need for formalities."

Closing her eyes briefly, she took a deep breath. "Hunter. This is my first night here. Can't we just get to know each other a little better before we do *that*?"

Raising a brow, he met her angry gaze. "Fuck you mean?"

Lila lowered her head but not before she shot him a glare. "You don't have to be so graphic."

"Should I pretty it up and give you some flowery speech?"

"All I want from you is to keep your promise." Her voice was low with an undertone of fury.

Yes, she'd be a hellcat in bed. The very thought of it had his cock jumping to life, straining against his pants to break free. Shifting in his chair to alleviate the ache within his throbbing balls, Hunter knew he wouldn't last much longer before taking her and burying himself inside her tight cunt.

He ran his tongue across his lips in anticipation. Would she taste as sweet as she looked? Examining her tightened lips and hands gripping the arms of her chair until her dark knuckles turned several shades lighter, Hunter realized he'd have to work at getting her hot.

It was a challenge he looked forward to tackling.

Chapter Five

"As long as you keep yours," Hunter finally answered. "Look, I've had plenty of lady friends before, but I've never been in an arrangement quite like this either, but it doesn't mean I'm willing to permit you to set the pace."

"But I'm sure you can understand my dilemma. I'm not used to jumping into bed with men I barely know. I'm only asking for a little time for us to be better acquainted before we sleep together." Lila hoped her plea would appeal to his good nature that was, if he had one.

Part of her wanted to run out of here and never look back, but what kept her planted in her seat, sitting across from this loathsome man, was thoughts of her father. After she'd told him Ramsey's wouldn't pursue buying his property, he'd seemed to lose all the worry clouding his eyes. He walked around with a spring in his step that had been missing for months and whistled, looking happier than he had in a long time. It was almost as if he'd gained several years on his life. Lila couldn't have his decline on her conscience, but still, how would she get through this ordeal without losing every ounce of self-respect she possessed?

"I gave you three weeks to back out of our agreement. But the very fact that you're here tells me you're fully prepared to honor your end of the deal. No. I won't allow you to brush me off now because you'll keep coming up with excuses as to why we should wait. In light of rearranging plans for the megaplex and in essence putting my business reputation on the line, you had better get used to the idea of sharing my bed, and fast.

And as for my sleeping with you, I have more productive things in mind than that."

Lila willed herself to remain still, otherwise she knew she'd slap the bastard into next week. If that was the way he wanted things to go down, she'd make sure she conveyed in every look, motion and sound that she didn't want to be here. She had agreed to allow him the use her of body, but he never said she had to like it. "Fine," she delivered between clenched teeth.

The sound of his chuckles tormented her. He was getting off on her misery!

"I like your spirit, Lila Saunders, but if this is to be a battle of wills, I'll have you know, I don't intend to lose. And no worries, my dear, there's no better way of getting to know each other than in bed. I look forward to the experience."

She kept her head bowed, refusing to rise to the bait. He may have had the right to her company, but there wasn't anything in their contract that said she had to enjoy it.

"Eat."

"I'm not hungry."

"Eat!"

She jumped as his roar reverberated through the dining room. Defiance raged throughout but to act upon her feelings would probably escalate things. Lila had a feeling that was exactly what the bastard wanted, so she focused her attention on the plate in front of her. As appetizing as her steak appeared to be, her stomach was too tied in knots to ingest a single bite. But still, if she didn't he'd press the issue. Lila didn't think she had the strength to continue the argument. She picked up her fork and stabbed a string bean with its prongs before popping it into her mouth. The vegetable could have been cardboard as far as she was concerned. She tasted nothing. "There. I ate."

Hunter watched her with those devastating green eyes, his expression giving nothing away. Would he take this as an act of disobedience? He lifted his wine glass and downed the remainder of its contents and stood up. "If you're through, then by all means, let's retire."

When he held out his hand to her, panic set in. There had to be a way to buy some more time. Lila shook her head. "Just give me tonight. I promise, I'll be ready for you tomorrow."

Nostrils flared as he narrowed his eyes. "Lila, I don't make a habit of repeating myself. Get up now or by God, I'll drag you upstairs."

"Sir, is there anything else you'll need?" Mrs. Coates poked her head into the dining room.

"Go away!" Hunter growled.

The older woman disappeared as quickly as she appeared.

Lila gasped. "Do you make a habit of talking to your staff that way? You are a hypocrite. How can you expect other people to be courteous to those who work for you, when you don't know the meaning of the word?"

For his answer Hunter grabbed her by the arm, practically yanking it out of its socket as he hauled her out of her seat and pulled her roughly against his body.

Her fighting instinct emerged. She didn't care what kind of bargain they had, there was no way she'd let him get away with manhandling her. Lashing out, she smacked his broad chest. "Don't ever do that to me again! You have no right—"

"That's where you're wrong, Lila. My house, my rules. You didn't have to agree to the terms set before you, but you did so now you'll have to deal with the consequences. So far my words have had no effect on you so I think the time calls for action."

Before she could utter another word of protest, Hunter bent over to lift and toss her over his shoulder like a sack of potatoes. The wind whooshed out of her lungs, making it difficult for her to speak. Stunned, she hung helplessly as he strode out of the dining room, took the stairs two at a time and carried her to a bedroom she assumed was his. Once her feet touched the floor again, her ability to talk had returned and she was pissed!

She gave him a shove. "Who the hell do you think you are? I'm not a rag doll you can lug around as you please. I may have agreed to be your companion for the next three months but I certainly didn't sign up to be abused by you, you fucking asshole!" If her father could hear her now, he'd be probably scold Lila for the language spewing from her lips. But then again, he'd probably be disappointed that she'd put herself in this position in the first place.

Hunter's response was to loosen his tie and shrug out of his black dining jacket. He was such a large man that her push had barely moved him. He seemed totally unaffected by her anger which only served to enrage her further.

"Did you hear me?" she yelled on the verge of tears. She couldn't remember the last time she'd been this mad, but this man had managed to drive her to rage with very little effort.

He unbuttoned his shirt, revealing a chest any bodybuilder would have been proud of. It was clear he worked out. Her gaze slid along the crested hills of his torso, sprinkled liberally with dark blond hair that trailed down the center of hard rippled abs. He'd seemed huge with his clothes on, but topless, he was a hulk.

Lila gulped, taking a step back. Shaking her head as though to deny what was happening, she held her hands out in front of her. "Don't."

He unbuckled his belt and pulled it out of the loops of his pants. "As we've already established, there's no backing out."

"No. You established it. I didn't. I don't think it was asking too much of you to give me a little time to adjust to this situation."

"But I believe it was. Just as it was a lot for you to ask me to rearrange my plans for a multi-million dollar project, which took weeks of finagling to get the board to agree to. I complied with your plea because I thought you to be a woman of your word. Was I wrong about you, Lila? Are you the type of woman who'll make pretty promises until she gets what she wants and then doesn't fulfill them?"

"No. When I say I'll do something I will..." With a groan, she covered her mouth. She'd basically backed herself in a corner. If she didn't go through with this, she would look like she was reneging and, judging from the smug smirk tilting those sensually curved lips, Hunter knew it too.

Damn him.

"That's what I thought." Kicking out of his pants, he placed his hand on the elastic band of his black boxers.

Lila shook her head, closing her eyes at the sight of his cock tenting his silk underwear. She wrapped her arms around her body, letting her mind wander to any place other than here. Once he touched her, there would be no going back. She'd be no better than a whore.

A cry escaped her lips when he reached out and grazed the side of her cheek with the back of his hand. She didn't expect his touch to be so gentle but she wouldn't let that sway her.

"Open your eyes, Lila. I won't allow you to pretend I'm someone else." Once again there was steel in his soft words, daring her to disobey his order.

Slowly she raised her lids, her insides churning with nerves. Why couldn't she stop shaking and dear Lord, why was he so—naked? Though she attempted to keep her gaze above waist level something drove her to look down.

Her mouth fell open. His dick was huge! It jutted forward, not a few inches away from her, long, proud and obscenely thick; she couldn't tear her eyes away from it.

"Do you like what you see?"

"No." The word had come out quicker than she intended them to making them a lie.

"The mouth says one thing, but the eyes don't lie. This is what you did to me. Have you any idea how many nights I've lain awake thinking about this moment? How it would be when I finally have you in my arms, and taking you anyway I'd like. I've even thought of a few positions that haven't been invented yet."

She looked away from his lascivious gaze but he grasped her chin between his index finger and thumb, forcing her to meet his stare. "You don't have to be so vulgar," she muttered.

He raised a brow. "Vulgar? What you call vulgar, I call honesty. I'm not going to sugarcoat my words to please your delicate sensibilities. This virginal act of yours doesn't go with the fiery vixen who came storming into my office."

Lila pressed her lips together tightly to keep herself from cursing at him. She hated that he could say these things to her and there wasn't a thing she could do about it. But what she hated most was that his dulcet tones seemed to be affecting her in a way she didn't quite expect.

"Cat got your tongue?" he challenged.

Still, she refused to reply.

His eyes darkened. "When you came downstairs for dinner, I could barely sit still. I'm so fucking horny, I can't promise our first time together will be as nice and slow as I'd like it to be. But I'll make sure you're satisfied by the time I'm done with you."

Lila narrowed her eyes. "I won't enjoy a single second of it."

That menacing smirk curved his lips. "Sounds like a challenge. I accept." Hunter pulled her against him, grinding his hardness against the juncture of her thighs before burying his face against her neck.

She stiffened. *I will not like this. He can do what he'd like to my body, but he'll never have all of me,* she silently vowed. He ran his hands up and down her spine as he peppered her neck with kisses. Lila willed herself to remain unresponsive to what felt like a pair of masterful hands, gently massaging her muscles. Unfortunately, her body wasn't in tune with her mind. To Lila's utter shame, warmth worked its way from her core and spread throughout her being at the gentle press of his lips on her flesh.

What had she expected? That he'd fling her on the bed, hump her a few times and be done? That's exactly what she'd believed.

Calloused hands slid across her shoulders and pushed the spaghetti straps of her dress down. "Beautiful brown skin," he murmured, caressing her with what almost seemed like awe.

A tremble made its way up her spine. No! This couldn't be happening to her. She didn't want to like this, didn't want it to feel good. Keeping her arms firmly at her sides, her fists clenched tight, she tried to maintain a steady breathing pattern.

Hunter pushed her dress to her waist with practiced ease. Lila wished she would have worn more clothing but that couldn't be helped now. Her nipples stiffened as the cool air hit them. He lifted his head and cupped her breasts. His thumbs grazed over the turgid peaks, bringing her to painful awareness of the stirring between her legs.

"Sexy. Like rich dark chocolate."

"Please" She whispered one last protest, not wanting to give in to the burning ache searing through her system.

"Oh, I definitely intend to." Hunter laughed softly and dipped his head to flick his tongue over one stiff tip, circling and teasing it until Lila began to shake uncontrollably.

Heat flooded her pussy, forming moisture in her panties. She bit her bottom lip to hold back the moan that nearly escaped.

Hunter pulled the burgeoning point into his hot mouth, sucking with fervent tugs.

Almost involuntarily, her hands found their way to his silky blond tresses, digging into them and holding his head against her chest. It had been so long since she'd been held and touched like this, and she couldn't believe how easily her body reacted to him. Lila pressed her thighs together to temper the heat pulsing between them. Hunter seemed to relish his task, taking his time and working her body into a frenzy.

He turned his attention to her other nipple, giving it homage, teasing and tormenting it until she whimpered from pleasure overload. He surprised her by dropping to his knees, taking her dress down with him until her garment formed a little black puddle at her feet.

Hunter jerked her panties down and nudged her thighs further apart, before burying his face between her legs, inhaling deeply. "Mmm. I love the scent of your arousal. You're so responsive. I like that."

Lila looked down to see he was eye level with her pussy. Why did he have to torture her this way? And why was she so turned on by the simple act of him staring at her?

"I'm glad you're not completely shaved down here. I like my women to look like women and not little girls and you're all woman, aren't you, Lila?" He brushed the nest of tight curls with the heel of his palm.

The warring emotions raging through her were making this ordeal more difficult to bear. Despite his skillful ministrations and her body's responses to them, she had to somehow get herself under control or she wouldn't be able to think straight. "Please, c-can't you just get this over with? I-I don't want this."

He lifted his head to look her in the face with knowing eyes. "I won't dignify that comment with a response, especially when you're so hot a trail of cream is running down

57

the inside of your delectable thigh." And to prove his point, he ran his tongue along the very line he'd pointed out.

Lila had to grip his shoulders to remain on her feet, otherwise her wobbly knees would have given out on her. Besides, she was still wearing the black heels she'd donned earlier, and it grew increasingly difficult to hold steady on them.

Parting the slick folds of her pussy, Hunter leaned forward and placed a kiss against her swollen clit and followed it with a long broad lick.

Her nails dug into his skin as she attempted to hold on to the last bit of her sanity. Lila could no longer kid herself. She wanted him. She was probably damned for feeling this way, but by God, the fire flowing through her veins could no longer be denied, especially when he sucked her hot nubbin into his mouth, his teeth grazing against it until she could no longer hold her excited moans back.

"Please." This time her impassioned plea was not for him to stop, but for him not to.

"Throw your leg over my shoulder."

He gave her no choice but to obey because he grasped her ankle and lifted it for her, his impatience evident. This time when he lowered his head, he attacked her pussy like a man hell bent on staking his claim, conquering—devouring. With his lips sealed tightly around her clit, Hunter eased his middle finger into her sopping-wet sheath, pushing knuckle deep. In that moment, she was lost. There was no turning back.

Thoughts of why she was here, her father, her vow to not enjoy this had fled completely. All that mattered was the irresolute desire rolling through her core and sliding along her central nervous system. "Hunter, that feels so good."

Lila ground her hips against the thrust of his finger burrowing inside of her. It was soon joined by another, stretching her walls as though she was being prepared for the intrusion of his cock. He used his mouth and fingers to lick,

58

suck and fuck her wet box until the slow buildup of passion exploded within her.

Her climax came hard and fast. Cream gushed from her pussy and Lila held on to him so tight, her nails furrowed into his skin, breaking it and drawing blood. Hunter seemed unfazed, continuing his onslaught.

Dizzy from what he was doing to her, Lila's could barely breathe as stars danced before her eyes. The man was after his pound of flesh and there was absolutely nothing she could do to stop him. "I can't take any more," she groaned, close to her second orgasm.

Hunter looked at her, green eyes blazing. "Oh, you will, my dear, and so much more." Pushing her leg off his shoulder, he stood up. Then he scooped her into his arms and carried Lila the short distance to his massive king sized bed.

"My shoes," she murmured, remembering she was still wearing them.

"Call it a little quirk of mine, but I find it highly arousing to make love to a woman in heels." Pushing her legs apart, he settled between her thighs and shoved his tongue between her slick folds.

"There's nothing more satisfying than feasting on a beautiful woman's cunt. I may not have had dinner, but this dessert more than makes up for it." He moved his palms over her belly, never lifting his head, until his hands reached her breasts, squeezing and shaping them.

Lila wiggled and writhed, mashing her pussy against his mouth. Never in her wildest imaginings would she have thought Hunter Jamison could make her feel this way, yet she was too caught up in a whirlwind of pleasure to care. There'd be plenty of time to deal with the fallout later. It wasn't long before she reached yet another peak.

Hunter lapped at her juices, slurping, grunting and savoring every drop. She was too weak to think coherently when she saw him rise to his knees. Grasping her thighs, he yanked her closer.

Closing her eyes, Lila refused to watch his final act of possession. Bracing herself, she clutched the down comforter beneath her as he pressed the bulbous head of his cock against her entrance, moving it up and down her slit, wetting it.

"Open your eyes, Lila. I've already told you, I won't allow you to pretend I'm anyone else. I want you fully aware of who it is inside of you."

Reluctantly, she complied, not quite looking at him but at some point beyond his shoulder.

He had been so gentle up until this point that it took her by surprise when he slammed into her balls-deep, filling her passage so thoroughly for an instant she believed he'd split her open.

"Goddamn you're tight. And so wet and ready for me." He uttered his words through clenched teeth as though he was having difficulty getting them out.

His fingers inside of her had been nothing compared to the feeling of being so completely stuffed by a thick hard cock. Not giving her much time to adjust to the sheer size of him, Hunter began to move, straining and pushing into her until it almost hurt, but it was the kind of sensation that hovered the line between pleasure and pain.

Her mind screamed this wasn't supposed to happen, but her body was in complete control. Lila gave over to the torrential heat consuming her. Grinding her hips, she met his cock as it plunged in and out of her. She gripped his dick with her pussy, tightening her muscles around him, causing Hunter to grunt incoherently.

They moved liked two dancers in a choreographed piece, so in sync with one another. She held on to him as they bumped, thrust and meshed their bodies together until Lila wasn't sure where Hunter began and she ended. This time when she reached her climax, it was more intense, raw and powerful. "Hunter!" The cry fled her lips before she could stop it.

"That's it, baby. Scream my name. Say it again."

"Hunter."

"Again."

"Hunter."

"Louder!"

"Hunter!" She yelled his name at the top of her lungs, making her throat burn.

"Oh God, I'm coming." Slamming into her one last time, he tensed before collapsing on top of her. He rested his sweat dampened forehead against her own as he gasped for breath.

As she slowly regained control of her hormones, reality smacked her in the face. She'd just allowed this man to use her body. What was worse — she'd liked it, couldn't get enough of what he'd done. Her shame was now complete.

Placing her hands against the hard wall of her chest, she gave him a shove with what strength she still possessed. Once she'd dislodged him, she rolled to her side, scooting to the edge of the bed as far away from him as she could get. Blinking hard, she tried to fight off the tears, but when Hunter touched her back, she lost it.

Stuffing her knuckles into her mouth, she muffled her sobs. Once she began crying, she couldn't stop. How could she have behaved like this? And how in the world would she be able to stop him from taking her again? Especially when she wanted him to?

Hunter removed his hand.

In her misery, she barely registered him rolling off the bed. It was only when a door slammed that she realized he'd left her alone.

Chapter Six

Pressing his hands against the shower wall, his arms holding him braced, Hunter stood under the scalding sting of the water's spray. He must have been in here for at least a half an hour. At this rate, he'd be a shriveled prune. But no matter the length of time he remained in the stall, the rage, sadness, and guilt would not be abated. Never had an experience with a woman touched on so many different emotions.

Holding and touching her had far surpassed the fantasy, but having her turn away from him at the end and cry as though her heart were breaking had been like a punch in the gut. Did he disgust her so much? Were his scars so hideous to her she couldn't believe she'd stooped to letting him have his way with her?

Hunter had been so sure Lila wanted him, too. Hell, he knew she did. The gasping moans, the way her body shook with just a stroke of his finger and the way her pussy had gotten so wonderfully wet couldn't be faked by even the most skilled actress.

Now that he knew what it could be like between them, one taste wasn't enough. He had to have her again. The very sight of how his pale hands had splayed across her dark body sent blood racing to his cock, stiffening it to near pain. He'd been with black women before, but out of the couple he'd dated, one had lovely cafe au lait skin while the other was not much darker than him. They didn't have Lila's rich cocoa hue. Not that they hadn't been lovely. They were. But they weren't Lila. Because there was such a huge contrast in their skin tones, Hunter never realized how something so simple could be an erotic turn on.

She was the epitome of perfection from the blue-black nipples cresting the well-formed mounds of her breasts to that pretty pink pussy, wrapped so tightly around his cock. He'd almost come the second he'd entered her.

For as long as he lived, Hunter would never forget how she'd made him feel. Being one with Lila had been like a dream, but then it had turned into a nightmare. His. At least the other women he'd taken to his bed since the accident pretended to enjoy the aftermath. Not Lila. She'd broken down completely. It had angered him at first. She had no right to pretend she was some vestal virgin who'd been taken by force. She'd been far from it. Hadn't he given her the opportunity to change her mind? Up until the very last minute, Hunter left her with the option to back out, but she hadn't.

Then, the shame had come. He wasn't the one who'd put her up to this. She was here for her father and he knew it. That's when the depression kicked in. While he'd fucked her, he could almost imagine she was there for him, not because he'd forced her hand.

With a sigh of resignation, he turned the nozzles of the shower off. Standing under rapidly chilling water wasn't going to change things. If he had any decency within him, he'd let her go home. But he couldn't, at least not until he'd had his fill of her and Hunter had a feeling that wouldn't be for a very long time.

Once he was dried off, he threw on the terry cloth robe hanging on the back of the bathroom door. He put his hand on the knob, but caught his reflection through the steam in the mirror. Walking over to it, he wiped the mist away. Hunter flinched at the sight of his scars.

Raising his hand, he touched them. It was no wonder Lila could barely look at him. He'd noticed it. There wasn't much about her that had escaped his attention. His fingers grazed the patchwork of imperfections criss-crossing the side of his face. When would the pain and desolation end? When would it cease to hurt so much? Was this to be his eternal punishment for the way he once used and discarded the women in his life? He wasn't crazy enough to believe any of them had cared about him beyond his wallet, so why him?

The right side of his face in its untouched state mocked him, reminding Hunter of the man he used to be. With a frustrated grunt, he turned away, his anger renewed. Lila wouldn't get out of their bargain by shedding a few tears. He wouldn't allow them to sway his decision in keeping her here.

Storming out of the bathroom with every intention of telling her so, the wind was knocked out of his sails when Hunter saw Lila lying in the same position she'd been in when he'd left her. She was curled up into a tight ball, her even, steady breathing indicated she was sleeping.

His gaze trailed down the curve of her back to her rear. He wanted to snuggle next to her, mold his body to hers, but didn't dare. Walking to the other side of the bed, he knelt in front of her.

Lila looked so vulnerable in this state, much younger than her twenty-seven years. Tear tracks stained her cheeks and again guilt briefly assailed him.

Hunter brushed aside a stray lock of hair that had fallen across her forehead. He used his knuckles to graze the softness of her cheek. In her sleep, she murmured something he couldn't quite make out before a small smile touched her full lips. Unable to help himself, he brushed their tempting fullness with his mouth.

When she stirred, he pulled back. It was probably best if he took her back to her own room. Besides, if she stayed in here with him, there was no way he could trust himself not to take her again. Nor did he have the stomach to wake up to her screams.

Hunter shuddered, remembering the last time he'd allowed a woman to fall asleep in his bed. After a night of sexual aerobics, he'd made the mistake of letting his guard down. When he woke up the following morning, Tina was still sleeping. Sliding on top of her still resting form, he'd planted kisses on her face and neck in hopes they would wake her.

The pure terror in her eyes was like a dagger through his heart. He'd never repeated that error again and he certainly wasn't going to do it with Lila. For some reason, screams coming from her would be far worse.

Careful not to wake her, he lifted her in his arms and took her to the room he'd designated as hers. Gently, Hunter eased her between the covers and dragged them up to her chin. For several moments, he stood, watching her sleep.

God, she was beautiful and for the next three months she'd be his for the taking. The sudden urge to wake her and slide his cock deep into her hot cunt again warred through him, but he pushed that feeling back.

He'd allow her a respite for the remainder of the night, because come tomorrow, there would be none.

Lila snuggled within the warmth surrounding her. Something cold and wet touched her face and then licked her lips. A pair of green eyes flashed in her mind and a delicious sensation heated her to the very core, sending little bursts of flames up her spine.

The damp stroke of what felt like a tongue grew more insistent. Why was he licking her face? She frowned not wanting to open her eyes, but then something spongy and moist nuzzled the side of her neck and sniffed. The sound of panting greeted her ears, followed by the scent of stale air that fanned her cheek.

What the hell?

She turned her head to evade the questing tongue and rank morning breath, but it didn't stop. In fact, it grew more persistent. Her lids popped open and Lila found herself staring into a pair of round, pale blue eyes.

Shooting up into a sitting position, she wiped her mouth with the back of her hand, her stomach suddenly feeling nauseous. Standing next to her bed was the biggest dog she'd ever seen. No, that wasn't a dog, it was a horse. Scooting away from the animal, she gagged. Yuck! While she liked dogs, it wasn't her cup of tea to be French kissed by one.

"Shoo." She gave it a gentle shove, but the four-legged monstrosity with its midnight coat wouldn't budge. As a matter of fact, it seemed to think she was playing a game.

Placing his huge paws on the bed, it climbed up beside her. Its mouth was turned into what looked like a smile.

"No. Bad dog."

But, it wasn't listening. Jumping up and down, he nudged her with his head.

Despite herself, Lila began to giggle. "You're just a big kid aren't you? A big hairy kid." She patted his shiny black coat and the dog preened at the attention.

"Miss Lila! I'm so sorry." Mrs. Coates rushed into the room. The housekeeper tugged the dog's collar. "Shadow, get down this instant. I guarantee this won't happen again. Usually, the dogs stay in the kennel when there is company or they're at Mr. Jamison's side. I think he caught the scent of a new person. Shadow is a people dog, I'm afraid."

Giving the dog one last rub, Lila smiled. "It's okay. He's a sweetie." She yawned. "What time is it anyway?"

"It's about ten past one."

"In the afternoon?"

"Yes."

Lila groaned. "I've never slept this late before in my life. I need to get up. It's no wonder I feel so lethargic."

"Take your time, Miss Lila. Whenever you're ready for something to eat, you can either come downstairs or I'll bring you up a tray if you buzz me on the intercom."

"I'll be down. I'm really not the type to laze around in bed all day."

The older woman shrugged. "I imagine you had a late night. Mr. Jamison said you were not to be disturbed."

Heat rushed to Lila's cheeks at the insinuation. Studying the housekeeper's face, she saw nothing malicious in Mrs. Coates's face. The statement was probably innocent, but it again reminded her of why she was here. No longer could she look Mrs. Coates in the eyes. Lila bowed her head, folding her hands in her lap. "That was thoughtful of him."

"Let me know if you need anything."

"Wait!"

The other woman halted mid-step. "Yes, Miss Lila?"

"Umm, is Mr. Jamison expecting me for lunch?"

The housekeeper frowned. "I don't think so. He usually stays in his office most of the day to work. He should be done by dinnertime."

"Oh." Then what the hell was she supposed to do all day? She wasn't used to sitting around idly. Would she be forced to stay in her room all day, bored out of her skull, waiting for him to be ready for her again? She trembled at the thought, but not from revulsion or cold. More from how she'd reacted to him the night before. Lila shook her head to rid herself of the carnal images of the night before from her mind.

"Is that all for now, Miss Lila?" Mrs. Coates broke into her thoughts.

"Umm, what am I supposed to do for the remainder of the day? Maybe I can help you around the house?"

Mrs. Coates's chin rose and her lips tightened briefly. "That won't be necessary. There's a library in the west wing if you like to read and the basement has been converted to a game room. The in-house theater is on the first floor and the weather is nice enough to take a swim if you're so inclined. I didn't get a chance to show you the place properly yesterday, but I'll be happy to do so today."

"Actually if you don't mind, I'd like to explore the place on my own...that is if you don't mind?"

"That should be fine, but please stay away from Mr. Jamison's office. He doesn't like to be disturbed while he's working."

"Which one is his office?"

"It's two doors down from the kitchen."

"Okay. Thank you."

The housekeeper gave her attention to the Great Dane who looked as though he was contemplating jumping on the bed again.

Lila shot him a look. *Not a chance buddy.*

"Come on Shadow." When Mrs. Coates closed the door behind her, Lila slid out of bed pulling a sheet off with her and wrapping it around her body. She wasn't used to sleeping in the nude. It suddenly dawned on her that she was back in her room. Hunter must have brought her here sometime during the night. As much as she tried to block last night from her mind, she couldn't.

All her intentions to not respond to his ardent caresses had been futile. He'd possessed her with the skills of a man who knew exactly how to please a woman. Images of his hands running along her body, tongue circling her skin, and cock stuffing her so fully, infiltrated her mind. Her pussy throbbed and nipples pebbled against the silk sheets.

No! She mustn't let that man get the better of her. It was only physical. Once the three months were over, she would walk away without a backward glance. Or could she? Strangely enough, she was experiencing something more than physical pleasure. If she wasn't, Lila might have been able to deal with these feelings, but no, it was something more — something she couldn't quite put her finger on.

He puzzled her. She had expected him to be rough with no regard for her pleasure, but he'd taken his time to make sure she was thoroughly sated, giving her not one, but three orgasms. No one had set her insides on fire like he had, yet there was no one she had more reason to hate than him. This ordeal was going to be much harder to get through than she'd originally thought.

Wanting to push all thoughts of the previous night from her mind, Lila headed to the bathroom to take a quick shower. Once under the spray, she made the water cool enough to wash up, but not warm enough to linger. She felt the longer she remained idle, those unwelcome thoughts returned. After taking care of her hygiene and dressing in a pair of jeans and tank top, she figured she could check up on her father.

She found her purse that had been tucked in one of the dresser drawers and retrieved her cell phone from it. Lila frowned when she noticed there were ten missed called. All of them were from Jason. She couldn't understand why he persisted in contacting her after she'd explicitly told him it was over. He was the one who'd basically called it quits when he gave her an ultimatum. And he was the one who took up with someone shortly afterwards. It wasn't Lila's fault that he suddenly had buyer's remorse.

She hoped that he'd eventually take the hint and leave her alone when she didn't return his calls. Lila called the apartment phone first knowing her father wouldn't answer his cell phone. Jesse Saunders was old fashioned when it came to technology and rarely remembered to carry the mobile device with him. Lila had to constantly remind him to keep it on him at all times, but it was a losing battle.

There was no answer. He was probably in the store at this hour so she tried that number but again he didn't pick up. Feeling a bit dejected she called the apartment again to leave a message on the answering machine. "Hi, Daddy. I just wanted to call and check in on you to see how you're doing. I'm getting settled in at this new job, but I already miss you so much. Take care of yourself and make sure to take your medication and lay off on the salty foods. I'll call again soon. I love you." With a heavy sigh she hung up.

With that out of the way, she squared her shoulders and took a deep breath, ready to face the beast.

Chapter Seven

It was difficult to get any work done while sporting a serious hard-on. Just knowing Lila was in the same house with him made his pulse race. Eager for the night to come when he could have her again, Hunter spent most of the day staring into space and rubbing his painfully engorged cock to ease the tension rather than focusing on his project.

He'd barely touched the food Mrs. Coates had brought in for lunch. What was Lila doing right now? Was she thinking of him? He snorted. Probably not. She was most likely counting the days until she could leave him. Why did that thought cause him pain?

His mind drifted back to last night and how she'd felt in his arms. Being inside of her had felt like heaven. She was so wet and tight Hunter never wanted that moment inside of her to end. And when he was finished, he'd been tempted to take her in his arms and hold her. It was a feeling he couldn't remember feeling for any other woman. Long before his accident he was a love them and leave them type of guy. Whenever he'd finish the act of sex, he'd usually dismiss his partner immediately, rarely giving them enough time to catch their breath. But after the accident, he was the one who left because he didn't want his lover to examine his face more than she had to. He'd made the mistake of lingering once before and didn't intend to do it again. But with Lila, he'd experienced something totally different.

Hunter had been on the verge of giving into his impulses and holding her until the wee hours of the morning, but then she started to cry. Her tears had shamed him. Was he that horrible to be with? Her outburst of emotion was enough to send him fleeing. By the time he'd gotten out of the shower, it hurt him to see that Lila had cried herself to sleep.

And then it occurred to him that it didn't matter what she thought about his looks. She was here to do what he told her. Maybe those tears had been a manipulation tactic to run him off. Well if that was the case then he wouldn't allow her to get to him again.

"It's just sex," he muttered under his breath. He would keep his feelings under lock and key from here on out.

Glancing at his watch, he noted it was going on five. Normally, he would get so engrossed in what he was doing that a lot of times he didn't rise from his desk until well into the night. With a frustrated grunt, he shut down his computer. There was no point in sitting here getting eye strain for nothing. Hell, who said he had to wait until dinner to have her again?

He was horny now!

If only he knew where the hell she was. Lila wasn't in her room, nor was she in the game room. Had she managed to leave without notifying him? Pain swelled within his chest. He knew she didn't care about him, but he could have sworn after last night she wasn't completely adverse to his touch. He walked into the closest bedroom and was about to press the call button on the intercom, but he saw Mrs. Coates coming down the hallway.

She inclined her head toward him. "Good afternoon, Mr. Jamison."

"Have you seen Miss Saunders?"

"No. I haven't see her since she came down for lunch and that was a few hours ago. She did mention something about visiting the kennel to see the dogs. I'm sure she's around here somewhere. If I see her, I'll let her know you're looking for her."

He held up his hand. "No. That won't be necessary. I'll look for her myself." The last thing he wanted was to appear too anxious.

She nodded and looked like she was about to move on but hesitated.

Hunter raised a brow. "Is there something you wanted to say?"

"No, Mr. Jamison."

Frowning, he wondered what could be on the woman's mind. In all the time she and her husband had been in his employ, she never gave her feelings away, but in the past couple days, he had the feeling she didn't quite approve of what was going on. "Are you sure?"

"Of course."

He couldn't force her to spill whatever was on her mind if she didn't want to share. Continuing on his quest, his anxiety was fast becoming anger. Was she hiding from him? He was about to pass the library when movement caught the corner of his eye. Sitting curled up in the far corner of the room with Shadow resting his head on her lap, was Lila. She seemed to be engrossed in her book while her hand absently stroked the dog's sleek coat.

Deja, his golden bull mastiff, lay at her feet. Usually, he let the dogs roam the house freely as they were both housetrained and caused very little mischief for dogs of their size. But when there were guests in his home, especially of the female persuasion, Hunter kept them locked in their kennel. In his experience, people were squeamish around large animals. Shadow was nearly two hundred pounds and Deja was one twenty-five. They were gentle creatures who wouldn't hurt a fly, but still intimidating in looks. Hunter had an affinity with them because people often judged them by the way they looked—kind of like him. So it amazed him to see Lila so comfortable with them. She was full of surprises.

Dear Lord, she was lovely. He'd found himself entranced by her beauty on several occasions, but each time he looked at her Hunter was fascinated how each emotion she experienced seemed to enhance her looks. When she was angry with fire blazing in the dark gold pools of her eyes, she was like an avenging fury. In her highest state of arousal, she was a sex goddess beckoning him to enter her Garden of Eden and sample her forbidden fruit. Now as she sat in calm repose, there was a calm about her, making Hunter want to cocoon himself within her warmth.

Unable to help himself, he took a step closer to the door. The movement brought both dogs' heads up. Deja and Shadow jumped to their feet and ran to him, their tails wagging. Hunter gave the panting animals each an affectionate rub behind the ears, but his gaze never left Lila.

She closed the book on her lap and wobbled to her feet, her expression wary. "I hope you don't mind my making use of your library, or letting the dogs out of the kennel. They didn't look too happy being cooped up behind that fence."

"I'd like your stay to be as comfortable as possible. Feel free to roam as you will. As for these two big babies, as long as you don't mind, I don't. Mrs. Coates keeps them in the kennel during dinnertime however, or they'll steal food off the table."

A smile turned the corners of her full lips. "Really? These two seem like angels."

He grimaced. "Trust me, you'd only get a few bites of your meal with these two around. Between them trying to swipe the food from your plate, they'll whine until you give in."

"Hmm, I guess that would get old pretty fast. They're gorgeous creatures. How long have you had them?"

"Three years. I got them when they were puppies. They were a great comfort to me after my—they're good dogs," he finished lamely. In a self-conscious movement he smoothed the hair covering his check. Never had he come so close to talking about his accident as he had just now—not that Lila would be interested anyway.

The simple fact he'd basically blackmailed her to be here with him told Hunter she would probably be repulsed by his ordeal. Even now she didn't quite look him in the face, instead keeping her attention focused on his dogs. Recalling how she'd turned her head when he'd tried to kiss her last night was all the rejection he could take in such a short period. There was no way in hell he'd open himself up to it again. He had to steel himself to not expect more from her than the limits of their bargain.

He ran his gaze over her jeans-clad figure. They were the same clothes she'd arrived in. "Is there a problem with the outfits I've provided you?"

Lila shifted on her feet, wrapping her arms around her body. "The wardrobe is lovely, but I…I don't feel comfortable wearing them."

Hunter furrowed his brows. He'd had the personal shopper pick out clothing from the top designers, nothing even the most discriminating of fashion plates could object to. "Not comfortable? Do they not fit?"

"They fit fine."

"Then what's the problem?"

She rolled her eyes heavenward. "If you insist I wear them, I will, but I'm a jeans and T-shirt kind of girl. Those clothes are far too beautiful for hanging around the house. Besides, when I was wearing that dress last night, which probably cost more than I earn in a month, I was so scared of spilling something on it."

"So what? Spills happen. You could have easily changed into a different outfit."

"That's the thing. I don't think I should have to. I don't like feeling this way."

"I see. If you're not happy with the items, I could have Ernest take you out tomorrow so you can buy whatever you like."

She shook her head. "That's okay."

"Don't worry about money. You can charge the clothes on my credit cards. After all, I did insist you not bring anything here but yourself."

"Because for some perverse reason you wanted to dress me up like a paper doll." The bitterness was clear in her voice. "If that's what you want then okay. I'll play along, but let's not pretend it was an act of generosity on your part. If anything, it's an attempt to control me. You always have to have the upper hand don't you?"

The mercurial mood swing took Hunter aback. The dogs must have sensed the tension in the room because they began to whimper. Her words were like daggers cutting into him. He hadn't sought her out to have an argument. But he wasn't going to let her to see how her obvious hatred affected him.

Narrowing his eyes, he gave her a long hard stare. "Seeing as how you think I'm trying to control you, I may as well live up to my reputation. I don't want to see you in that outfit for the remainder of your stay. Dinner will be served in an hour. Wear something appropriate and don't keep me waiting like you did last night."

Lila folded her arms beneath her breasts. "Or what?"

"Or I'll paddle your ass raw."

Her mouth opened, eyes widening. "You wouldn't dare."

"I don't issue idle threats, Lila. Six o' clock...and choose something sexy."

"I hate you"

"Hate me all you like, but for the next several weeks you'll follow my rules or would you rather call the whole deal off?"

For a moment, she looked like she wanted to do just that. With her fists balled at her sides, Hunter believed if he were standing closer to her, she'd probably belt him one.

"It's easy for you to challenge me when you know I have no recourse. Fine. You win, but so we're absolutely clear with each other, you make me sick to my stomach. Whenever you touch me, my skin crawls."

Hunter laughed out loud to show her barb hadn't been like an arrow to the chest—even though it was. "How easily you forget the way you screamed my name last night and clung to me like you couldn't get enough of what I was giving to you. I believe I need to jog your memory." He advanced further into the room, stalking toward her like a panther with an eye on his prey.

Though she took a step back, Lila wasn't quick enough to evade his grasp. "Let me go!" She struggled against his hold.

Hunter slammed her against him, crushing her breasts between their bodies. He moved to capture her lips, but she turned her head. "Don't!"

He grasped her ponytail and gave it a healthy tug, exposing the silken column of her neck. "You're in no position to dictate my actions." He circled her beating pulse with the tip of his tongue. At the small contact, her stiff body relented and she began to tremble.

The hands that had been pressed against his chest, poised to push him away, fisted in the folds of his shirt. Releasing her hair, Hunter allowed his hands to slide down her back to cup her ass and gave it a squeeze.

Lila moaned, her eyes widened, but the expression he read within them wasn't one of outrage, but arousal.

Hunter moved his hand between their bodies and undid the button of her jeans and then unzipped him. With that barrier out of the way, he wedge his hands inside her panties, grazing the soft hair between her thighs. "I can already feel your heat, sweetheart. I bet you're nice and wet for me. Just like you were last night."

Lila caught her body lip between her teeth as her eyes glazed with an unmistakable emotion. Lust.

Hunter grinned. "Cat got your tongue, baby?" He rubbed her slick folds before slipping a finger inside her depths. Just as he suspected, she was wet and ready for him. He was easily able to slip in another finger. Her pussy clenched around his digits and Hunter could only imagine how amazing it would feel with her pussy wrapped around his cock.

Lila gripped his shoulders with a groan. "Dammit," she muttered.

"Feels good doesn't it," he taunted as he slowly eased his fingers in and out of her. He used his thumb to simultaneously graze her clit.

Her response was a low moan.

Hunter shoved his fingers deeper and harder inside of her. "I didn't quite get that. You like this don't you?"

"You know I do." Her head fell on his shoulder as she tightened her hold on him. She moved her hips in time with his finger. "But this means nothing."

"You can say that even though this tight little cunt is weeping for my touch? You can lie to yourself, but don't ever lie to me."

He continued to finger Lila's pussy, working her body into a frenzy. When he felt her body stiffen, he knew she was close to her climax." It occurred to him to pull away and deny her the release as punishment for her defiance, but then that would rob him of pure bliss on her face and the satisfaction of knowing he was the one who'd put it there. He pressed down on her clit which sent her over the edge. Hunter held on to her as shuddered in his arms. Her warm honey coated his finger and hands. Slowly he removed his hand and made Lila watched as he licked her cream from each finger.

His cock was painfully stiff. More than anything he wanted to toss her to the floor and bury himself deep inside her tight sheath, but knowing Lila wanted it too was enough to get him through dinner. He released her with an abruptness that had her stumbling backwards.

Righting herself, Lila glared at him, her eyes narrowing. "I hate you so much."

"You keep saying that, sweetheart, but your body doesn't. Are you going to deny the ease in which I made you come? And by the way, you taste delicious." He chuckled to drive his point home. Hunter didn't really want to taunt her. Hold, kiss, caress and worship her body was what he wanted to do. Not this bickering. Hell, this was only her second day here and they were already at each other's throats. He didn't want things to be this way between them, but what else could he have expected?

A little more amiability? Perhaps he'd envisioned—no. Hunter knew how it would be between the two of them when they made their bargain. There was no point in dwelling on the should've, could've, would'ves. But, why did he feel so empty inside?

Lila's glare became venomous. "Maybe my body does want you, but it's only that, my body. My mind, heart and soul don't."

"Fortunately for me, then, your body is all I require. I'll see you at dinner." Turning on his heels before she could make another retort, he strode out of the room with the dogs following him.

That man! One day she'd bring him to his knees and he wouldn't know what hit him. It was extremely inconvenient to respond sexually to him even when she knew what kind of man he was, the type to plow over those with less money and power than him. A man who felt he could do or say what he wanted because of his position in life. Strangely though, in her brief stay in his home, she caught glimpses of another side of him.

Lila couldn't quite place her finger on what it was, but then again, did she care? Should she? Probably not. She couldn't remember being this confused about anything in a long time. When she was younger, she used to run to her father and he always seemed to know the right things to say.

If only she could hear his voice now, she'd feel so much better, so she decided to give him a call, hoping he'd be in the apartment and not in the store. She cursed herself when she realized her phone was dead and she'd forgotten to bring her charger with her. Whenever she was allowed out of her gilded cage, she'd have to buy another one. Fortunately there was a landline in her room.

Hunter hadn't said she couldn't make calls on his house phone. Once she was in the safety of her room, Lila's hand trembled as she punched the numbers, her heart pounding when the other line began to ring. Even if her father wasn't there, hearing him on the answering machine would have to do. At this point, she would take any crumbs she was offered.

"Saunders' residence."

Just to hear him brought tears to her eyes. More than anything she wanted to be there with him while he held her and told her everything would be alright. Too choked up to get the words out, her lips moved soundlessly.

"Hello? Who is this?" he prompted. "If this is a prank caller or a telemarketer, I'm hanging up."

"Daddy, it's me."

"Baby?" His pleasure in hearing her was evident and it made her feel better.

"Yes, it's me. H-how are you?"

"I'm doing fine. I just woke up from my afternoon nap."

"Since when have you started napping?"

"Doctor's orders. Your old man is getting up there in years, baby girl."

"That's nice to hear you're finally listening to the doctor. If I knew this would happen, I would have gone away sooner."

"Well, I did some thinking and I want to be here for you as long as I can. Anyway, I got the message you left. I tried to call you back but the call just went to voicemail."

"Oh, my phone died and I forgot to pack my charger. When I get the chance to get another one I'll keep in contact more regularly."

"That's good. But you don't have to worry about me. Before I forget, your young man has called a few times. Said, he wants to get in contact with you but you haven't been answering your phone."

Lila rolled her eyes. She hoped this young man wasn't who she thought it was. "Dad, I don't know who you're talking about. I'm single."

"You know that nice young doctor, you were seeing. Jason."

She groaned. Why the hell was he contacting her father all of a sudden? She would have thought he'd have enough pride to know when he wasn't wanted. It wasn't her problem that things didn't work out between him and Veronica. "Dad, we've broken up. If you see his number on the caller ID, don't take the call. He's been an absolute pest but I'm hoping he'll eventually take the hint and leave me alone."

"That's too bad. He seemed like a really nice guy."

"That's just one of his faces, anyway, enough about him. I want to hear how you're doing."

"Well that nap didn't certainly hurt. Can't remember when I had one in the middle of the day with running the shop and all."

"So I take it all is going well."

"Yes. Those teenagers working in the store have been very helpful. They hardly let me do anything. It's given me a chance to work on the books. And that nurse you got for me came by today. How is your patient doing?"

Patient? Then Lila remembered how she'd lied to him about her reason for being here. "Fine. He's f-fine. I—" A sob tore from her throat and she broke out into noisy tears.

"Baby? What's the matter?"

It took several moments before she could regain her composure. She felt like a fool for worrying him like this.

"It's okay, Lila. Get it out, you have to. Daddy's here."

"It's just—I miss you so much and wanted to talk to you."

"Are you sure? You've been away from me before. Tell me what's really going on. You haven't cried like this since you were a child."

"It's..." Did she dare tell him the truth? Knowing how much pride her father had, he'd probably make her come home. Then what? He'd lose the store for sure. She should have waited to get herself together before calling him. "I know, but I had a bad dream last night that something happened and I just wanted to make sure you were okay." The lie didn't come easily, but she hoped it sounded convincing to him.

"Child, I'm fine. That nurse makes a bigger fuss over me than you and like I said, Reg and Carla are good kids if not a little talkative. Gloria is coming over tonight with one of her casseroles."

"Mrs. Perez?"

"That's the only Gloria I know. She's a nice lady."

82

Lila grinned. Her absence might not be such a terrible thing for him after all. Jesse Saunders was still a good looking man. It came as no surprise to her that he still got his fair share of attention from the ladies. Lila liked Mrs. Perez so she was glad her father would have some companionship in her absence.

"Tell her I said hello."

"Will do. Is everything going well with your job? Do I have to kick someone's ass?"

She giggled, wiping the tear streaks from her face. "Now that I know you're alright, I am too."

"Is your employer treating you well?"

Lila paused for a moment before crossing her fingers. "As well as could be expected. This isn't the typical patient. He's…very moody." It wasn't exactly an untruth.

Jesse chortled. "I'm sure you'll have him eating out the palm of your hand by the time your assignment is over. You can charm the bees from honey."

She snorted. "Hardly. You have much more faith in my abilities than I do."

"Since you were small, you had something in you people flocked to. Some people have it and others don't. You have it, baby girl. And if your boss can't see it, then there's something wrong with him."

Lila wondered what her father would say if he ever came face to face with Hunter. "It's not really a matter of me being charming. I'm here to do a job and that's it."

"Hmm, then why do I get the sense there's something going on you're not telling me?"

She closed her eyes against the lie she knew she'd have to tell. "I guess I'm a little stressed is all. My, uh patient is more than a little moody at times. He can be an absolute beast and there's only so far my charm will go with him. When he wants something, he expects me to do it immediately, or else."

"Used to getting his own way?"

"Definitely."

"Does he have any family or friends who visit?"

"Not that I'm aware of."

"Maybe he's simply a lonely man who isn't used to social interaction."

It was so like her father to try to see the good in other people. Lila doubted he'd find many redeeming qualities in Hunter Jamison. She toyed with the idea of telling him the reason why she was really here and being done with it. As much as she hated lying to him, Lila dreaded disappointing him even more and this would definitely qualify as that. "You could be on to something. He's had a really bad time recovering from his injuries."

"It could be one of the reasons he's so moody as you put it."

She snorted. "I think he was probably a jerk long before the accident."

"If that's the case, then this can't be easy for him. And haven't I taught you better about judging people? You never know what someone else is going through unless you walk a mile in their shoes. Maybe what this guy really needs is a little understanding. I know he's a client, but maybe what he really needs is a friend. Maybe you should try a little harder to see things from his perspective."

Could her father be right? Was she being too hard on Hunter? Maybe what Hunter really needed was a little understanding, but would he accept an olive branch from her? Lila had made damn sure Hunter knew her only reason for agreeing to their arrangement was for the sake of her father. Should she have been so blunt? Perhaps he was just as ashamed of their deal as she was. After all, it must have been quite an ego crusher for him, a former playboy, to resort to blackmail in order to get what he wanted from a woman. That he even had to was kind of sad. Confusion assailed her. She wasn't supposed to feel sorry for someone she'd vowed to hate. Lila shook her head to rid it of her guilty thoughts.

She and her father chatted idly for another few minutes before he had to get back to the store. The conversation had made her feel much better, but it didn't change matters. She still had three months to put up with "The Beast" himself. It would be a miracle if she could walk away from this mess unscathed.

Chapter Eight

Tonight she chose a cream off the shoulder dress which dipped to the small of her back. The skirt rested mid-thigh. The fine material crested over her curves like a second skin and Lila had to admit she looked good in it. But she couldn't shake the feeling of being some kind of mannequin dressed for Hunter's pleasure.

Glancing at herself in the full length mirror, Lila ran her fingers through the hair that fell to her shoulders to assure her appearance was in order. She'd stalled as long as she could. It was time for dinner.

"Miss Lila?" Mrs. Coates's voice chimed in over the intercom.

Lila rolled her eyes, realizing she was being summoned. She walked over to the offending box on the wall and pressed the talk button. "Yes, Mrs. Coates?"

"Dinner will be served in five minutes."

"I'm on my way down."

"I'll let Mr. Jamison know."

"I'm sure you will." Lila spoke softly, but she heard every word.

"Did you say something, Miss Lila?"

Damn. Her finger was still on the button. Still, the woman had bat ears. "Umm, no."

"Very well. I'll see you shortly."

Lila felt like she was in grade school all over again and teacher had caught her passing notes. There was no point in delaying the inevitable. She had to face Hunter sometime. With an impending sense of doom, she trudged down the stairs and walked to the dining room.

Hunter was waiting for her. He stood when she drew close, his bright eyes gleaming with naked appreciation. She didn't want to be pleased by his blatant desire for her, but a tingling sensation spread through her body.

"You look lovely tonight."

Keeping her lids lowered as she took her seat, she gave him a brief smile. She didn't see why they couldn't at least be cordial to one another. "Thank you."

If it was his intention to play nice, she was willing to go along with it. Frankly, all the bickering was starting to wear on her nerves and she hadn't even been here that long. Lila didn't like the hostile feelings she harbored toward this man, even if he did deserve them. Perhaps for her own peace of mind it was better to try and get along with him rather than look for an argument. Her father's words came back to her and Lila steeled herself to get through the rest of this night with as little conflict as possible.

Hunter sat once again, taking the bottle of white wine and pouring some into her glass. "Try this. I think you'll like it."

"I'm not—" It was on the tip of her tongue to tell him she didn't want any, but she stopped herself. If she was going to get through the next several weeks with her nerves intact, arguing with Hunter wouldn't be the way to go.

She brought the glass to her lips and took a sip. She wasn't much of a drinker but this wasn't bad. In fact, the mixture of fruity flavor with just a hint of sweetness was pleasing to her taste buds. "It's very good."

"I'm glad you like it. It's from my vineyard."

Lila raised a brow in surprise. This was news to her. "I thought you were strictly into property development."

"That's my main interest, but my fingers are in several pies. For instance, I'm part owner of a car dealership, several restaurants and various businesses."

"You must stay pretty busy if you're running all of those things."

"I don't do it all on my own. There are people who work under me who see to my business holdings."

"Figures," she muttered before taking another sip of wine.

He stared at her from over the rim of his wineglass. "What's that supposed to mean?"

"Nothing." Lila silently cursed herself for letting her mouth get ahead of her thoughts. If she didn't want to start any arguments with him she'd have to guard her tongue more carefully.

"Are you by any chance surmising that I sit on some kind of throne while the worker bees do everything for me?"

She shook her head vehemently. "Not at all. Forget I said anything."

"I assure you, Lila, I don't demand anything of my employees that I'm not willing to put out myself," he continued as if she hadn't spoken. "A company can't run properly if it has a weak link in the chain and as the leader, it's my job to keep that chain strong. Most days, I'm working from dawn until well after midnight."

"That can't be healthy."

He gave her a lopsided grin. "You actually sound like you care."

"I guess it's the nurse in me. I'd feel this way about anyone."

He raised his glass and brought it to his lips and took a sip before saluting her with it. "Honest to a fault. If I had any ego before you arrived, I certainly won't have one for very much longer."

Lila nibbled on her bottom lip. There she went again, putting her foot in her mouth. She would get this conversation on better footing if it killed her. "I didn't mean it that way. And of course I'm genuinely concerned. You're not doing your body any favor by working such a grueling schedule."

"Probably not, but work is all I've had since..." His eyes narrowed slightly before he took another sip from his wine glass.

"The accident?" For the first time since she'd joined him, Lila looked at his face. His hair which he still wore parted in the middle and hanging down on either side of his head obscured most of his scars. She could still see angry red lines peeking through, however.

They weren't so bad, compared to some of the things she'd seen throughout her career. Probably having one side of his face still untouched was a constant reminder to him of how he used to look. If the society papers were correct about his former playboy lifestyle, having half of his face disfigured would be harder to deal with for him than it would have been for other people.

She could tell how self-conscious he was about it by the way Hunter was constantly patting his hair down over the marks, which is what he was doing at this very moment. Didn't he know it only drew more attention to him? Lila would have pointed this out, but the last thing she wanted was to make him feel more insecure than he already was.

"It's all right if you don't want to talk about it. I'm sorry I brought it up."

"You didn't. I did. And yes, I've worked more hours since my accident, but I worked a lot before it so I'm used to it."

Mrs. Coates appeared, wheeling in a cart with their dinners and then proceeded to serve them.

The Chicken Francese lined with roasted potatoes and asparagus had Lila's mouth watering. She didn't plan on making the same mistake twice by not eating dinner. "It looks delicious."

The older woman nodded. "Thank you, Miss Lila." She turned her attention to Hunter. "Will that be all?"

He nodded his head in approval. "Yes. Thank you."

Only after the housekeeper was gone did Hunter reply to her last statement. "To answer your question, my work has pretty much been my life since the accident."

"Why do you hold yourself away from the rest of the world? Maybe people make such a big deal about your face because you do." She cut into her chicken, attempting to add a casualness to her voice she didn't quite feel. The last thing Lila wanted him to think was that she was trying to get into his head. That was always the fastest way for people to shut down. A lot of people thought that a nurse's job was simply providing medical care to patients and doing the things that were beneath a doctor, but her job required so much more than that. Patient care involved patient involved getting to care of a patient's physical and mental health. She found that sometimes just talking to a patient often made them feel better.

Hunter stiffened, his fork halfway to his mouth. "You seem to have it all figured out don't you?"

Lila took a sip of her wine before answering. "It's pretty obvious. For instance, you keep your hair in your face. That probably draws attention rather than detracts from it."

Hunter didn't reply. Lila could have kicked herself. She'd resolved not to mention what was on her mind and did exactly that. This wasn't a good time to suffer from run-of-the-mouth-itis. But for a moment Lila had caught a sad look in his green gaze which had touched something deep within her. In that moment there was much more to him than just the business tyrant or the scarred recluse. There had to be something charming about him. How else would he have earned the reputation of ladies' man before his car wreck? She wondered what he was like before then.

Lila cleared her throat and began her next attempt at conversation. "What do you like to do besides work? Do you have any hobbies?"

"No." The answer was curt and Hunter offered no further elaboration.

The remainder of dinner was eaten in silence, only broken when Mrs. Coates would come in to check on them. By the time dessert had come around, the tension was so thick it could be cut with a knife. Lila couldn't take it any longer.

"Hunter," she began tentatively, "I won't bring it up again if it bothers you. I didn't mean any offense. I was only…"

"Making small talk?"

"No. Well, yes. But seeing as how we're stuck together for the next three months, we may as well get to know each other better."

He placed his fork down and leaned back in his chair. "Say what you really mean, Lila."

She frowned. "What are you talking about?"

"You said we're stuck together. What you meant was *you're* stuck here with me. Isn't it?"

Lila shook her head. "I said what I meant. You're twisting my words."

"Am I? So in other words, if I weren't holding something over your head you'd be here on your own volition?"

"Probably not." The words spilled out before she thought about how they may have sounded.

Hunter's lips twisted into a grimace. "That's what I thought."

"I didn't mean it as it sounded. No, I probably wouldn't be here because our paths probably wouldn't have crossed otherwise. I'm hot dogs and beer. You're caviar and champagne."

"Very nicely put, but let's not pretend you meant anything other than what was said. I appreciate your honesty far more than your lies."

"Okay, maybe I did mean it that way but I didn't mean it to come out so harsh. And anyway, even if we did move in the same social circles, I wouldn't want to be here because of your actions, not the way you look. You have to admit, your reputation wasn't particularly stellar before your injury. And the fact you were trying to destroy something my father and me held dear didn't make you a recipient of the good guy award, in my book. I wouldn't care if you looked like a movie star, I'd still not want to be here, but since I am we may as well make the best of it."

Green eyes narrowed. "So looks don't matter to you?"

"Not particularly."

He rolled his eyes, disbelief etched in every line on his face. "Go ahead and pull the other one. You may have fooled yourself into believing that bullshit, but you sure as hell haven't convinced me."

"That's because you care so much about them, it puzzles you when someone else doesn't."

"Says the woman with the face of an angel. I bet you've had things pretty easy all your life because you're beautiful."

She shrugged. "So what? You think because of the way I look I've never face adversity? I have. I'm a woman of color in American, not everything is a cake walk. Besides, I can't tell you how hard it is to be heard because people automatically assume I'm stupid. And trust me, just because you think I'm pretty doesn't mean everyone does. I was teased when I was younger because kids said my lips were too big and my skin was too dark or my hair is too kinky. But eventually I had to learn to love the skin I'm in."

"That may be all well and good for you, but I'm sure whoever said that about you was simply jealous. Me on the other hand…when people call me a monster and point out these hideous scars, it's because they're actually ugly."

Lila threw her hands up in the air in frustration. "Well, I guess there's nothing I can say to make you see things my way."

He leaned back in his seat and studied her with his intense stare as he absently swirled the wine around his glass. "There's no need to pretend with me if they do. It won't make any difference one way or another."

"It's the truth. I'm not that shallow."

"Then you're one in a billion. I've found more women of my acquaintance would rather cross the street when they see me coming than look at my face. I can't see how you're any different."

"You must be exaggerating." He had to be. Or was he? Perhaps that's why he was so bitter. No one deserved to be shunned the way he had, even if karma had finally caught up to him. Lila squirmed in her seat, suddenly uncomfortable with this sympathy she was beginning to feel for him. The last thing she wanted was to care, to see him as a human being who hurt like everyone else. Getting along was one thing, but understanding was quite another.

"Am I? I can't have imagined the look of horror in my lover's face when the bandages came off. You see, the irony of the whole situation was, she was in the vehicle during the accident. We argued because I wanted to end the affair. She'd grown a little too clingy for my taste. Dawn, on the other hand, thought we should take the relationship to the next level. She made such a scene in the restaurant, I had to take her home." He paused for a moment and gulped the remainder of his wine down.

93

Lila could see the pain radiating out of every pore in his body and it touched a part of her she didn't expect. She sat silently, waiting for him to continue.

"When I was taking her home, she cried, yelled and begged for another chance, but it grew tedious very quickly. I was so agitated with her tears and protests of love that I didn't notice that drunk fool driving down the wrong side of the road. Fortunately for her, she survived with a few minor abrasions, while I lay in a hospital bed for weeks in pain, bandaged like a mummy, not knowing how extensive the damage would be. Dawn came by to visit diligently and I was grateful for her company. I even began to think maybe she did love me as she'd claimed to. I'd certainly never given credence to that word before, but I started to depend on those visits. I even fantasized about a possible future with me and Dawn." He closed his eyes briefly as if having difficulty getting the words out.

Lila's heart ached for him. She wanted to wring this superficial woman's neck for callously discarding Hunter at his most vulnerable. Lila most certainly could never have treated anyone so cruelly. "You don't have to finish."

He shook his head. "I want to. Besides, if you're so eager to learn about my life, you might as well hear the bad. Where was I? Oh yes...then came the unraveling and I don't think I need to go into detail, but, she couldn't get out of the hospital fast enough. She, of course, said she'd be back, but it was the last time I saw her. I should have guessed right away, but I found out later she'd moved on to the next shlub—an heir to a toilet bowl company."

"Then obviously she didn't love you. She wouldn't have been able to walk away so easily otherwise."

"No shit."

"You can't lump all women in the same category just because one woman did you wrong."

"She wasn't the only one, just the first in a line of many. When word spread I was single again, my exes appeared in droves thinking they would be my Florence Nightingale, until they got a look at my face. I may have been able to handle the rejection a little better if it wasn't for how other people would treat me. It got to a point where I couldn't go to my office or out in public without looks of fear and disgust. I might have gotten past that, but I couldn't take the pity. I made a small child cry once."

"That's horrible." Lila wanted to offer words of comfort, but she knew he'd probably take them as pity.

He laughed humorlessly. "For the child, I'm sure."

"No. For you. I can't imagine how you must have felt."

"Of course, you can't. Because a person like you has probably had it easy. No matter what you said. So what if people think you're stupid before they even speak to you. Clearly you're not. But even if you were you'd get treated 100 % better than someone who isn't attractive. Most beautiful people do. I took my looks for granted until I lost them."

"I don't spend time obsessing on how I look, Hunter. I have too much going on in my life to do that. Besides, as I've already people out, with so much hatred in the world, doesn't it stand to reason that I've been judged by the color of my skin? It doesn't feel good, but the people who do that to me aren't worth my time."

"I concede there are small minded people in the world, but it's not exactly the same. I'm sure there are more people who admire the way you look than not."

"Again, it's way too trivial to dwell on."

"Then you're a rare human being if you don't think looks matter."

Lila shrugged. "I'm not so naive to think they don't with most people and I acknowledge there has to be some degree of attraction between two people if they want some kind of

95

relationship, but in the grand scheme of things, the surface doesn't matter much. What counts is how a person is on the inside. One of my favorite quotes is 'beauty fades, but dumb is forever'."

Hunter's lips turned up in a half smile. "Is that something your father taught you?"

She grinned. "No. Judge Judy. But she had a point. If I had to choose between the two, I'd much rather be smart than pretty."

"Says the beautiful woman." His voice dripped with scorn.

"You're the one who's got a hang up about my looks, not me. Anyway when it comes right down to it, once you get used to a person you want more than just a pretty face. You want a little substance. When I finally settle down, I'd rather be with a man who makes me laugh and is a good person rather than a man with Hollywood good looks who is a jerk. Been there and bought the t-shirt. It's not an experience I intend to repeat." Her mind drifted to Jason with that last statement.

"You actually sound as though you believe that drivel you're speaking."

"It's not drivel. And I do believe it." She was beginning to get a little annoyed. Lila wasn't used to anyone questioning her integrity or trying to find double meaning in her statements. "Anyway, you're not completely innocent either."

"Oh?"

"Yeah, I've seen some old articles about you in the society pages. I've never seen you with anyone who didn't look like a supermodel. So don't sit there and pretend like you've never judged anyone based on their looks. I bet there are plenty of genuine women who wouldn't care about your wealth or position, but you didn't give them the time of day because they didn't have perfect bodies, or they weren't up to your standards of beauty. You reap what you sow and if you chose to date nothing but gold diggers, you can't expect them to be around in your time of need."

Blood rushed to Hunter's face, turning it a deep shade of red. His nostrils flared and he flexed his fingers as if he was contemplating strangling her. But finally after a moment of tense silence, he relaxed. "Perhaps." Hunter leaned forward. "Tell me, Lila of the noble heart, why did you cry last night? You sit there with your Pollyanna attitude of the world while you can't stand to look directly at me. And let's not forget that you passed out the first time you got a good look at me. Oh, you claim it was because you hadn't eaten but we both know it's a lie. You're no better than the other women I've come across. In fact you're worse. You're a hypocrite. The worst kind of woman."

Lila slammed her hand on her the table. "Don't compare me to the trash you used to date. They may wear expensive clothes and mingle in the highest of social circles, but they lack the one thing you can't buy and that's class. And I don't appreciate you calling me a hypocrite."

"I'm just calling it like I see it. They at least were more upfront. Everyone has a price, Lila. Some women are just more expensive than others. If you were honest with yourself you'd realize you have one as well."

She took the napkin off her lap and threw it on the table, her appetite gone. All resolve to make it through this dinner with little conflict flew out the window. This man had to be one of the most obstinate people she'd ever met. It was no wonder he'd been dubbed The Beast, although she could think of a few more titles that would suit him even more. "I don't have to sit here and take this."

"Oh, but that's where you're wrong. And I see you've neatly skirted around my original question."

Lila stiffened. "What question?" She knew exactly what he was referring to, but admitting her reasons why would be her final humiliation. She should have known she couldn't get away with that fib. Hunter was much too shrewd not to guess.

His lips twisted and eyes flashed his disbelief. "You're trying my patience, Lila. I don't make a habit of repeating myself, but I'll ask one more time: why did you cry last night? Were you so disgusted by me you couldn't take it or is it a habit of yours to weep after sex? If it is, it's not much of a turn on."

"It's not something I ordinarily do."

"Then answer my question." He spoke with such dead calm, it sent a chill down her spine.

"I-I can't." As much as he'd just angered her, telling him the truth would probably hurt him and it wasn't in her to do that to him.

"That's what I thought. You make pretty speeches, but they don't mean jack squat. You're starting to sound tedious and I'm getting tired of it. When you speak to me, you're looking everywhere but my face." He pushed his hair behind his ears, revealing the full extent of his disfigurement.

Lila flinched, but not because she feared him, but because it saddened her as she imagined how horrible it must have been for him to suffer as he had.

"You say my scars don't matter, so prove it. Come here and kiss me."

Why did he have to ask of her the one thing she couldn't do?

"Look at me, Lila." His voice was soft but the underlying steel in his tone left no doubt in her mind that his statement wasn't a mere request.

Tears stung the backs of her eyes at the raw pain she heard in his words. She didn't want to look at him the way he ordered her to because then she'd start to care as she feared she was very close to doing so anyway. She couldn't afford to care.

"Look at me!" he roared, making her jump.

A tear escaped the corner of her eye which she hastily wiped away. Lila shook her head. "Don't make me."

"You'll fucking do as you're told. I've had enough of your defiance and if you don't do as I say, by God, I'm going to make you!"

Chapter Nine

Hunter leaped out of his chair, rage guiding his movements. He'd had enough of her lies. She wouldn't meet his gaze yet she chose to stand behind her lie. Lila was like the rest of the women in his acquaintance. No. She was far worse because she'd nearly had him believing that bullshit she'd been spouting.

He yanked Lila out of her seat and led her out of the dining room, moving so fast she had no choice but to follow him, otherwise she would have fallen.

She tried to pull away, slapping at his arm. "Stop this right now, Hunter! It doesn't have to be this way."

He turned to shoot her a glare before continuing on. "Yes it does. I promised you punishment and now it's time to pay the piper."

"No! You misinterpreted my words. If you would have given me a chance to explain why I couldn't do as you asked then maybe you'd calm down."

"Don't bother. My bullshit tolerance is extremely low, and I'm not in the mood to hear any more of it."

Digging her heels in, Lila halted. "What do you plan on doing to me? A-a-are you going to spank me?" she croaked.

Hunter smirked. "As tempting as that sounds, I've thought of something much more fitting. For every action, there's a consequence and you're about to find out what yours is."

"Hunter if you go through with this—"

"What? You'll hate me? I've heard that before, remember. It's time you came up with some new material." For a brief moment, he caught a glimpse of what looked like fear swimming in her eyes. Guilt surfaced inside of him. She had to know he wouldn't hurt her physically. But he wouldn't relent on what he planned on doing. He would make her eat her words. "I would rather you hadn't tested me on this, but you've made your choice so now you'll have to deal with it."

Lila's struggles renewed. Hunter wrapped his arms around her waist and carried her the rest of the way to his bedroom. He dumped her unceremoniously on the bed and then walked over to his closet and pulled out a box he hadn't used in ages.

He looked over his shoulder to see her watching him, her expression wary. "What is that?" Her eyes darted from side to side as if she were staking out an escape route.

"You'll find out soon enough."

She tried to scramble off the bed, but he intercepted her, using his body as a blockade.

"You're not going anywhere." Hunter opened the box and removed a length of nylon rope and then tossed the container aside.

Lila took a step back. "I won't let you tie me up."

Instead of answering her, he laughed menacingly. "Take off your dress."

"No." She moved further away from him until her back hit the wall.

Hunter placed the rope on the bed and slowly made his way toward her not stopping until he was only a few inches away.

She held up her hands. "Okay. I'll do it." Her anger was palpable.

"I'm glad you're beginning to see things my way," he taunted.

"Do I have a choice? If I refused, you'd find a way to bully me into it anyway."

"Don't try to worm your way out of this."

"I'm only voicing the truth. You're a bully and I despise you for it."

"You're starting to sound like a broken record. Do you keep saying it to convince me or yourself? Perhaps you do hate me, but you love what I do to your body, don't you?"

She placed her hands over her ears. "Shut up!"

He grabbed her arms and pulled them down roughly. "Hit a nerve, didn't I?"

Lila lashed out at him, her palm connecting with his cheek.

Hunter closed his eyes against the sting of her blow, almost welcoming the physical pain to replace the internal torment.

She gasped, her hands flying to her mouth. "I'm sorry."

"I'm sure you've been itching to do that for a long time, haven't you?"

"I still shouldn't have done that. I abhor violence." She trembled and he wondered if it was because she was truly sorry for what she'd done or because she was scared of what he might do to her because of it.

"I don't want your apology, I want you to undress. Do it now!"

Her lips quivered for a moment and she raised that stubborn chin of hers again before reaching behind her and unzipping her dress. She pushed it down until it fell at her feet. Looking straight ahead, she balled her fists at her side not attempting to cover her naked flesh.

Hunter's dick sprang to attention at the sight of her delectable naked body. It was insane how he could want a woman as much as he did her. "The panties, too."

Lila hesitated for the briefest of seconds, but then complied.

He couldn't tear his eyes away from the magnificence of her feminine curves, but he wouldn't allow them to sway him from his course of action. He had to show her who was boss, teach her a lesson. For all the people who'd shunned him, the women who'd hurt him, Lila was the embodiment of them all. So beautiful on the outside, but inside she harbored the heart of the biggest hypocrite.

"You're no different from anyone else. When these three months are over, you'll go back to your life and feel better about yourself because you did a noble thing. I know your kind, Lila Saunders. You're a do-gooder out tilting at windmills and preaching your 'We are the World' bullshit. And in the meantime, you sit around patting yourself on the back, wondering how these ignorant people could have possibly gotten along without you. I think it suits your martyr complex to be here right now, doesn't it? Going toe to toe with the Beast? Do you see yourself as some kind of savior? You're no better than me."

Her mouth opened slightly then closed before she spoke. "That isn't true."

"Of course it is. Even now you can't stand the sight of me, but that's okay, because I intend to break you out of the habit." He retrieved the rope from the bed. "Give me your wrists."

Hunter expected her to argue, but instead her shoulders slumped and she slowly presented them. Still, she wouldn't look at him. That only served to piss him off.

Taking her wrists, he wrapped the rope around them. It had been a long time since he'd included this in his sex play, but with her tied to the bed, she couldn't turn away from him

103

so easily. Once he was sure the knots were secure, he led Lila to the bed. Where had her fight gone? Why didn't she protest?

"On the bed," he ordered.

Again, she complied without another word. Hunter took the end of the rope and looped it around the post, raising her arms above her head.

She lay completely motionless, her lids lowered. He realized the game she was playing. He wouldn't stand for her passive-aggressive defiance and he knew just how to deal with it.

Once the rope anchoring her arms to the bed was tied to his satisfaction, he undressed with hurried motions, anxious to possess her. He vowed by the time he got through with her, Lila would know who the master of her body truly was. Standing naked, Hunter perused every inch of her frame, contemplating where he'd start first.

He sat down beside her, the bed depressing under his weight, and stroked her cheek. "Look at me," he whispered softly.

"You have me where you want me and the power to do anything you'd like. Why do you have to keep pushing the issue?"

Hunter clenched his jaw muscle. The gauntlet had been tossed and this was a battle he intended to win. He grazed her flat stomach and then cupped one well-shaped breast. Lowering his head, he flicked her nipple with the tip of his tongue. The little bud came to life, puckering to a taut peak. He took it fully into his mouth and then fondled her breast in his palm.

"Oh," Lila sighed, her body writhing beneath his ministrations.

His body tightened at her responsiveness. He loved her naturally passionate nature. Tugging the hard tip between his teeth, Hunter applied enough pressure to make her cry out, but not enough to cause serious injury.

Lila's skin was so soft and tasted so good. Hunter gave her other breast the same treatment until Lila was moaning incoherently, her body wildly wiggling.

Hunter lifted his head then. "Look at me."

She squeezed her eyes shut, but he wasn't about to give up. He'd have her surrender by the end of the night if it killed him. Slipping his arms underneath her body, he flipped Lila onto her stomach.

He then pulled her to her knees, forcing her to use her restraint as leverage. She began to tremble. Her apparent fear wasn't something he wanted, but at least it was an honest emotion. Deep down, he wished it could be different between them, but he was the one who'd made the rules and he'd have to abide by them.

Running his hand down the curve of her back, he didn't stop until it rested on the seat of her ass. "You have beautiful skin. When I first saw you, this is what I wanted to do." He placed a light kiss on her shoulder then pushed her hair aside and pressed his lips against the nape of her neck.

As he moved his mouth over her satiny skin, Hunter slid his hand between her legs, pushing them further apart. The inside of her thighs were wet. A small smile touched his lips when he saw this evidence of her arousal. Even if she wanted to fight him, her body would always be her Judas.

He dipped his finger between the cleft of her pussy and rubbed her dewy clit.

"Hunter," she moaned, squirming against his touch.

"That's it, sweetheart. Say my name. Know that I'm the one who's doing this to you," he whispered against her skin. He rolled the hot button between his thumb and forefinger.

Lila bucked her hips. "Oh God!" She tugged at her restraints as though trying to break free, but Hunter knew it was her fiery nature making her writhe so wildly. It was one of the reasons he'd tied her up in the first place, because a woman as passionate as she would barely be able to stand being bound, unable to use her hands as she willed.

Hunter knew his touch was driving her wild and he loved seeing her so turned on and ready to be fucked. The very scent of her arousal was driving him to the brink of insanity. He'd set out to conquer, but feared he might be the one to succumb to her charms.

He removed his fingers and grasped her ass, spreading her cheeks apart as he studied the beauty of her tight hole resting above her pussy. One of these days, he'd take her in that forbidden place, but tonight he had other plans. Eager to sample her fragrant cunt, he moved behind her. Parting her slick folds, he shoved his tongue into her tight passage.

"That feels so good," she sobbed, pushing back against his mouth.

Hunter slid his tongue in and out of her channel as he reveled in Lila's tangy, musky and tantalizing flavor. He could easily get drunk from the very taste of her.

Her body started to shake and he realized her climax was near. Though he wanted to continue, Hunter pulled back.

"Please don't stop."

He ran his tongue over her pussy lips to capture the last bit of her cream and sat back, watching her suffer with wanting him.

"Hunter?" Uncertainty making her voice wobble.

"Yes?"

"Why...why did you stop?"

"It's part of your punishment. You don't come until I say you do."

"And when will you say?"

"When you beg for it."

She gasped her outrage. "I won't."

"But I think you will."

"If you believe that, then you'll have a very long wait."

Hunter smirked. "Somehow, I doubt it." Sliding his fingers into her pussy, he pushed them deep. He could tell she was fighting the urge to respond but soon gave in just as he knew she would.

Lila relaxed her stiffened stance and moved against his thrusts.

Hunter fingered her slowly and then leaned forward and whispered in her ear. "All you have to do is say the words and this can be my dick. Admit you want it, or I swear I'll stop."

She bit her bottom lip. It was obvious she was trying to decide what to do. "Yes," she finally spoke so softly he could barely hear her.

Hunter hadn't realized he was holding his breath until the tension from waiting on her answer eased out of his body. "I didn't hear you."

"Yes!" she yelled, her resentment clear. "Just stop torturing me. I want you. There. Are you happy?"

He was certainly getting to that point, but he was much too horny to gloat. With a swift movement, he flipped Lila on her back again and pushed her knees apart. Without hesitation, he positioned his cock at her entrance. "Look at me."

When she turned her head, he wanted to pull back, but knew he would be hurting himself as much as her. Hunter pushed into her tight channel with a loud grunt.

Her walls tightened around and gripped his shaft, sucking him so deep, he felt like he would shoot his load right away. His eyes squeezed shut, he moved within her, relishing the feel of her.

"Hunter."

Hearing his name on her lips was like music to his ears. He opened his eyes and noticed hers were still shut. Something within his snapped. A primal urge to demonstrate his supremacy took over.

He slammed into her so hard, Lila cried out. Hunter continued to plow relentlessly into her, fucking her with a combination of lust, anger and a perverse need to make her pay for making him feel inadequate—like a hideous monster she couldn't bear to look at.

Despite his rough savagery, she moved with him, taking all he dished out until her body tensed and shook. Lila cried her climax. Her pussy gushed around his cock, but Hunter wasn't finished with her, not by a long shot.

Gripping her face to ensure she couldn't turn her head away from him, he rode her even harder. "Open your eyes."

When they remained closed, he forced her hand. "Open them!" he bellowed, clenching her face in a vise. "Now!"

Slowly her eyelids rose.

"Do you see me? I'm the one who's fucking and giving you pleasure. Take a good look at me Lila. Can you honestly say that looks don't matter now?"

She didn't answer, but the unshed tears in her eyes said it all.

Releasing her face, Hunter screwed her until his orgasm hit him like a series of fireworks going off in his body. He shot his seed deep inside her hot hole. As he gasped for breath, he rolled off her, horrified at what he'd just done.

Why had he let his temper get the best of him? Despite what he thought of her, she didn't deserve his rough treatment and shame kept the apology lodged in his throat.

Lila lay so still beside him, Hunter wondered what was roaming through her mind. She was probably wishing she was anywhere but here with him at the moment.

He moved to a sitting position and untied the rope from the bedpost. She offered her wrists without being asked and he undid the knots. Hunter then rolled off the bed and grabbed his boxers off the floor, quickly donning them.

It took him a moment to speak as he searched for the appropriate words to say. What could he say after what he'd done? With a frustrated sigh, he raked his fingers through his hair wishing he could go back in time to before he'd ever met her, and then at least he'd have most of his sanity still intact.

"I assure you, this won't happen again," he began gruffly.

If he was any kind of gentleman, he'd let Lila out of their agreement, but he couldn't bring himself to say the words. The very idea of her walking out of his life and never seeing her again caused him pain. It was ridiculous feeling this way about someone in so short an acquaintance, but Hunter knew if she left, it wouldn't be something he could get over easily.

"My behavior was inexcusable and for that, I apologize. If you would like to stay in this room tonight, I'll go to one of the other bedrooms, or you can return to your room whenever you're ready."

Lila sat up, massaging her rope-burned flesh. For the first time since she'd arrived, she was looking at him without his directive. "I think I'd like to stay here for the night—with you."

Chapter Ten

Hunter took a step back, shaking his head as if he couldn't believe what he'd heard. "What?"

Lila climbed off the bed and stood in front of him, tilting her head back to stare at him directly in the face. One of the main reasons she'd avoided looking at him for so long was because she knew she'd be forced to throw out her preconceived notions about this man. In her mind, Lila had wanted him to remain a tyrant—not a man who hurt and experienced emotions like anyone else. Now that she'd seen this side of him, she could no longer treat him with the indifference she'd set out to do.

Hunter flinched at her boldness. Inwardly, she chided herself for having behaved so cowardly. In a way, she was glad he'd forced her to take a good look at his face in full, scars and all, because it gave her a glimpse into his tortured soul. She could no longer ignore his anguish, the pain lurking deep within him. There was something inside of him which touched her in a way she didn't think possible. A connection was made she couldn't quite put her finger on, but it was there nonetheless.

It had probably been there all along, but she'd been so hell bent on fighting it. Now there was nothing left but to deal with these feelings brewing inside of her. Did he feel the bond between them or was it only one-sided on her end? Perhaps the question she should have asked herself is, was she insane? This man was supposed to be her enemy. There should be no tender emotions toward him. Yet there were. By no means did she think it was love, but it was something nonetheless.

Lila would be with him for the next three months and she might as well stop fighting Hunter every step of the way. From now on, if there was to be any conflict between them, it wouldn't originate from her. She placed her hand against his chest. "I said I would rather stay here with you."

His gaze roamed her face. He was probably trying to figure out whether she was serious. Abruptly, Hunter turned his back on her. "I don't want your fucking pity."

She pushed away the urge to match his anger. Breaking the barrier he'd erected between them wouldn't be easy. Besides Lila realized he'd be suspicious of her motives. Since she'd come to his home she'd told him in not so many words of the contempt she felt toward him. Of course he'd question the sincerity of her change of heart. There had to be some way she could reach him. "That's good because you won't be getting any from me."

He snorted. "Then why the sudden about face?"

"Could you please turn around and look at me while I'm speaking to you?" The irony of her words wasn't lost on Lila.

"Why? Haven't you had your fill of me already? Do you want to stare at the freak some more?"

The man had more barriers than Fort Knox. She circled him until they were facing each other again. "You probably don't want to hear it, but I'm sorry for how I acted. I mean, yes I was resentful about being here, but it has nothing to do with how you look."

He rolled his eyes in his apparent disbelief. "Go ahead and pull the other one." Hunter turned his head to show off his scars.

Lila suspected he did that to deliberately put her off, but she wouldn't let him. Not anymore. For some reason it had become important to her convince him he wasn't the monster he believed himself to be.

She could tell Hunter was still determined to call her bluff. There was only one thing she could do. Capturing his face between her palms, Lila stood on her tip toes and kissed his lips.

Hunter stiffened, remaining immobile as she moved her mouth over his. She ran her tongue along the seam of his lips before pushing it past his teeth to fully explore the cavern of his mouth. His taste was so wonderfully male, she deepened the kiss. She'd never been so forward with any man before and she found the experience of taking the lead titillating.

With a groan, Hunter wrapped his arms around Lila, giving in to her insistent kiss. His tongue met hers in an erotic dance. He ground his lips over hers as if he was afraid to let her go.

Lila pressed her body against his, twining her fingers through his loose blond locks. Heat surged through her and she wanted him all over again, but this time it would be different. She'd let her defenses down.

He was no longer the man she'd grown to dislike. Hunter Jamison was simply a man and she was a woman; two people who were in desperate need of a little compassion and loving. She was the one who finally broke the tight seal of their lips, but only to catch her breath.

Then, she kissed his jaw line on his scarred side.

"Lila," he growled softly.

"Shut up, Hunter. I'm in charge now," she shot back before touching her tongue to where her lips had been. Lila refused to let him deter her from what she intended to do. Running her hands over his hair-roughened chest, she slid her fingers down until they encountered his cock.

He was rock hard.

"Lila, I don't know what kind of game you're playing..."

112

"This is no game." She moved down the length of his toned torso to his ripped abs and then went to her knees. Wrapping her fingers around his thick rod, she touched the velvety smooth hood with her lips. With her free hand, she cupped his throbbing balls and fondled them lightly. "Do you like this, Hunter?"

He inhaled sharply. "You know I do," he groaned.

She glided her lips along his cock and sucked him into her mouth, one delicious inch at a time, not stopping until its tip touched the back of her throat. As she bobbed her head back and forth, Lila continued to squeeze and play with his tense sack.

Hunter moaned out loud, placing his hands on either side of his head. "What are you doing to me, woman?"

She pulled back, releasing his cock with a decisive, wet pop and looked up at him. "Making you feel good, I hope."

The hunger in his gaze told her that was exactly what she was doing. His heavy breathing was all the confirmation she needed. Lila licked his rod along the side before taking it back into her mouth.

Giving him pleasure filled her with a blistering heat that surprised her. She hadn't expected to feel this way. Her pussy was on fire. Needing to ease some of the ache burning between her legs, she released his balls, and speared her pussy with two fingers, working them inside her channel in cadence with her mouth moving over his cock. Her movements grew frenzied as the intensity of her arousal increased. She sucked him harder, fingering herself deeper.

Hunter's grip on her head grew firmer as he guided it along his dick. "Lila, I'm going to come." He tried to pull away, but she wouldn't let him. "Lila!" he yelled hoarsely.

His seed filled her mouth and she attempted to swallow as much of his essence as she could. She was so close to her own orgasm, she shoved another finger into her passage, stretching it until an explosion ripped through her body.

113

He reached down and hauled her against his body, then crushed her mouth beneath his. His kiss was hard and hungry. She didn't notice they'd moved until she realized Hunter was laying her on the bed.

She eyed his erect cock in amazement. "You're ready for me again?"

Covering her body with his, he slid easily into her wet hole. "Did you think after that I could leave you alone?" His gaze roamed her face with tenderness lurking within its depths.

Something twisted inside her heart as he began to move inside of her. "Come here," she whispered.

He pressed his body into hers and she wrapped her arms around his neck and her legs around his waist. This time their coming together transcended fucking and mere sex. It was something different entirely, as though their souls were coming together. He was so gentle, Lila felt like crying all over again, but not from anger, pain or shame, but because of the deep connection she felt with him in this beautiful moment.

Lifting her hips to meet him thrust for thrust, she moved and strained against his body. Her nails grazed the back of his neck. When Lila came yet again her climax gave her peace. A wave of contentment flowed over her.

Hunter pushed in and out of her for several more strokes before reaching his climax. Resting his forehead on hers, his breath mingled with hers. "That was amazing. You were amazing," he whispered.

A smile tugged the corners of her mouth, exhaustion making it difficult for her to reply verbally. Hunter was heavy, but she welcomed the pressure of his weight, pressing her into the bed. It felt right for some reason.

He was the one to break the silence, lifting his head with wonder in his eyes. "Why?"

She brushed the side of his face with the back of her hand. "Why not?"

He captured her hand and gave it a squeeze. "Don't."

"I thought you enjoyed my touch."

His expression grew stormy, his bright green eyes turning a deep jade. Hunter rolled off her and sat up, shaking his head which made his hair fall into the style he usually wore it. "I told you I didn't want your pity."

Lila joined him in a sitting position, wrapping the comforter around her body. She'd need to be patient with him if she wanted to break through the wall he'd erected around himself. "Hunter, after what just happened, do you honestly think what I did was out of pity?"

He raised his shoulders in a shrug. "I don't know what to make of what you did. One minute you can't look at me, and then the next you can't stop. What am I supposed to believe?"

If she was to gain his trust, Lila knew she'd have to be honest with him. "You'll probably think I'm silly, but the reason why I never looked at you was because I didn't want to think of you as a real person. As nutty as this sounds, in my mind, I had you built up as some monster who was trying to destroy everything I held dear. And before you get defensive, I'm not referring to your face. I hated you, or at least I thought so before I learned of your accident."

"Because of your father's store?"

"Exactly. Deep down, I always knew what your company was doing isn't something new, or anything another property developer in your position wouldn't have done, but Ramsey's was going after something I loved and the stress was damaging my father's health. If it weren't you, my anger would have been directed to whoever was in charge, but I had to fight. Maybe you're right about one thing. I probably do have a do-gooder complex. In my wild imaginings, my father and I were the victims and you were the villain."

"I see, but that still doesn't quite explain everything."

She placed a hand on his arm. "Please let me finish."

"Okay, but I still don't understand."

"'I guess I'm not explaining myself very well. Basically, when we received that last letter from your company, I thought you were a completely reprehensible man to do something so underhanded. It gave me this preconceived notion of what you were like. Coupled with all the stories of your playboy lifestyle, I even began to believe you deserved what happened to you."

Hunter flinched at her statement. "Perhaps I did. A lot of my business associates and women I've dated would probably agree with you."

"But I was wrong. Don't misunderstand me. I'm still willing to fight tooth and nail for my father's business. I just believe my way of thinking was a bit overboard. When I stormed into your office that day, I wasn't really prepared to see your scars, but when I did, they made me angry, they humanized you, gave you a vulnerability I didn't want to associate with you. I saw your pain and then I knew if I kept looking at you I wouldn't be able to hate you as I had before. I couldn't compartmentalize you into a neat little body. Knowing this, I tried not to look at you because I was afraid of caring about you. And before you ask, I fainted because I hadn't eaten all day."

Hunter furrowed his brows. "Are you saying you care about me?"

"No. I'm saying I could, and that's what I was fighting so hard against."

She brushed the hair on his face aside and touched his scars, wanting him to know she wasn't frightened of him. "I don't want to fight with you anymore, Hunter. I'd like us to be friends."

His mouth slanted into a half smile. "Are you by any chance trying to wiggle your way out of sleeping with me?"

She laughed. "I don't think that would happen even if I tried."

"Damn right it wouldn't."

"I don't want to stop." Heat rushed to her cheeks and Lila felt shy all of a sudden.

"Lila if you're messing with me…"

"I'm not. I'd like us to be friends. Since I'm going to be here, we might as well try getting along outside of bed as well. Is this something you'd be agreeable to?"

Hunter stroked his chin. "I've never had any female friends before."

"Maybe that's why your relationships didn't work in the past. Women are more than playthings and so am I. Look, I know our arrangement isn't conventional, but we might as well make the most of the situation."

"Ok. Why not? Do you really not care about the way I look?"

"Your scars take some getting used to, but they don't define the person you are. I'm a nurse and trust me, I've seen a lot worse. I once had a patient who'd been a victim of a gunshot wound to the face. I won't bother getting graphic about it, but I'll always remember that kid. He was only sixteen when it had happened, but he was always upbeat and positive. It makes one appreciate their own life. When you think you have it bad, remember, someone always has it much worse."

"When put like that, you probably think I'm a shallow son of a bitch."

"A little."

He scowled. "Your honesty is going to take some getting used to."

117

"Friends are honest with each other."

Hunter's gaze roamed her face for several moments before he replied. "You're really trying to push this friendship thing aren't you? I'm surprised you'd want to tangle with the Beast?"

"I wouldn't call you that, although I'm still annoyed about the city council getting involved."

Hunter exhaled deeply. "Honestly, that was the work of an over-enthusiastic executive who thought he could score some points that way. It's not normally how I do business."

"But you taunted me about it when I confronted you."

"And I'm sorry for it. My day wasn't going well, and I'd only just learned what that executive had done."

"Would you have really gone through with it?"

"To be truthful, Lila, I don't know how I would have dealt with the situation and now neither of us ever will because you chose that very day to storm into my office. But I will say it's not a tactic I've ever used before. In most cases, Ramsey's usually builds in abandoned areas or on vacant land."

"But not this time."

"No. But as we were planning, we tried to find an area which would displace the least amount of people. I can't apologize for that."

Lila appreciated his honesty, but it was still a sore topic for her so she decided to change the subject. "How did you get such an awful nickname anyway?"

"When I took over Ramsey's, I felt I had a lot to prove because most of the employees felt I didn't deserve my position."

"Why not?"

"One of my stepfathers took me under his wing. At times, I was probably more aggressive than I should have been, but

118

my business decisions often got positive results for the company, hence the nickname."

"Ah, your stepfather used to run this business." She at least understood how he'd come to work for the company he now ran.

"Yes. Ben had no children of his own and he was pleased when I wanted to learn the business."

"You said stepfathers in the plural."

"Yes, I've had a few growing up, but I'm sure you don't want to hear my life story."

"I wouldn't mind. It would give me some insight into the man himself, and maybe I'll understand this chip on your shoulder in regard to women."

"I don't have a—"

"Yes you do, and it's the size of a boulder. Spill it."

"Are you sure I won't bore you to death?"

She winked at him. "As long as you resuscitate me if I show any signs of dying, I think I'll be okay."

"If nothing else can be said about you, you're definitely a persistent lady, Lila."

"So they tell me. Now stop stalling."

"Truthfully, there's really not much to tell. I had a pretty average childhood until my father died when I was ten."

"I'm sorry. I only had my dad growing up, so I know what it's like to only have one parent."

"You, at least, had the advantage of being close to your father. I'm sure Mom cared about me as best she could, but she wasn't the most maternal of women. She wasn't the kind of woman who liked to be alone. She remarried within three months of my dad's heart attack. She was—is—an attractive woman and has never been short on male attention. I guess I grew a bit resentful at how quickly she was able to move on while I was still grieving."

"Do you think that's where your mistrust of women began?"

"I won't say I mistrust women entirely. In my experience, unfortunately the ones I've had dealings with were more interested in what a man could give them rather than the other way around."

"We're not all like that. I'm not."

"So you keep saying."

"Because it's the truth."

"Hmm." He neither agreed or disagreed.

Lila silently counted to five before she spoke again. She had to remember it would take time for him to get over his hang-ups. "What happened when your mother remarried?"

"My first stepfather wasn't a bad guy. Ben was as good to me as any man who'd had a ten year old stepson suddenly thrust upon him. He'd even offered me the Ramsey name. I refused out of respect for my father though. I was just starting to get used to the arrangement when Mom decided she couldn't handle what she called his workaholic attitude. I was fourteen then."

"That's a shame."

"It was upsetting, but Ben and I kept in contact in the following years. Stepfather number two was a widower with a daughter. He resented the hell out of my presence and made no secret of it. Being a self-made man who'd come from nothing he liked to throw his money around, making sure everyone knew how much he shelled out for everything. Ted made sure I realized I was in his house because of his largesse. I hated him for constantly putting me down but I started to despise my mother even more for letting him. In retrospect, I didn't exactly demonstrate model behavior."

"But you were a teenager, he was a grown man."

Hunter's lip quirked briefly. "You're very generous."

"I'm just calling it like I see it. Did you get along with your stepsister at least?"

"Karen didn't make matters easier for me."

"She teased you?"

"In the worst way a girl could do to any hot-blooded teenage boy. She loved to show off her body, flashing me when no one was looking, and touching my knee and rubbing my crotch under the dinner table."

Lila gasped. "How old was this girl?"

"Seventeen and very developed. I didn't stand a chance. I don't think I have to tell you what happened next. She came on to me and I took what she offered. Unlucky for us, or me rather, we were caught. Ted gave me an ass kicking I'll never forget for taking advantage of his innocent angel." He snorted. "She wasn't a virgin when I had her, but she was always so well behaved around him."

"But she was older than you—knew better. Surely he could see she was just as responsible.

"Karen could do no wrong in Ted's eyes. Hell, she even turned on the waterworks and said I'd forced her. That earned me another pummeling, although I did get some nice shots in myself. Anyway, I was sent to boarding school after that incident because he refused to have me under his roof anymore. Mom stood back and said nothing as usual."

"You can't hold women responsible for what your mother and some *girl* did to you. Whatever happened to them by the way?"

"Last I heard, Ted made some bad business deals and went bankrupt. I hear Karen got knocked up from some soldier who abandoned her. I believe she's married to a pastor and they have six or seven children. Ted lives on their charity which is a fitting end to him. I hear they're both miserable according to my mother."

"Do you have a relationship with your mother?"

"Not really. I hear from her occasionally when she remembers she has a son. She's currently married to a guy who owns a couple of car dealerships. They travel a lot. The last time I saw her was shortly after my accident. She took one look at my face and cried. She made small talk and then pretended she had somewhere else to be. Sometimes she sends a postcard from wherever she. She calls on my birthday. That's about all the contact with have."

"Well I guess it's something that she remembers your birthday."

He shrugged. "I suppose."

"Don't judge all the women based on those bad experiences."

"Maybe I shouldn't but I haven't seen any shining examples of female virtue. After I took over Ramsey's for Ben and made it what it is today, all the attention from the women went to my head. In my mind, I was getting a little of my own back for past hurts. I didn't give a lot of them a proper chance to find out who was using me and who genuinely liked me. They were all the same to me. My earlier experiences hardened me against the fairer sex. I suppose my accident didn't help matters. Until tonight, I didn't realize how bitter and angry I'd become at people, the world and myself." He took her hand in his. "I don't want to be this way anymore. I want to heal. Teach me how, Lila."

Her heart went out to him. Hunter's impassioned plea touched a part of her she didn't believe he was capable of. Her response was to lean over and offer her lips him.

With a groan, Hunter lowered his head to accept. For the first time since her arrival, Lila didn't feel homesick.

Chapter Eleven

Lila touched his sleeve, compassion etched in every line on her lovely face. "If you're not comfortable coming out, I don't mind if we get takeout and go back to the house."

Though she kept her voice light and casual, Hunter could hear the anxious undertone of her words. Ever since he'd decided to take her out for dinner, he couldn't fight the nerves coursing through his body. Going to work and dealing with his colleagues was a trial in itself, but it was a necessity. This on the other hand was different, voluntarily putting himself out there to be scrutinized by the public, inviting the stares, trying to ignore the whispers behind cupped hands. Perspiration beaded his forehead when he thought about it.

Clenching his fists to prevent his hands from shaking, he pasted a smile on his lips. Lila had turned out to be everything he could possibly want in a companion, and more. Because he hated seeing that look of abject longing he saw in her eyes when she didn't think he was watching, Hunter had suggested they go out for a night on the town. To say Lila was thrilled at the suggestion was an understatement. Throwing her arms around him, she'd thanked him profusely and Hunter knew there was no turning back.

How could he tell her he'd changed his mind, when he hadn't seen her face light up like that before? Hunter hadn't realized how much making Lila happy meant to him until that moment. As much as he wanted to tell Ernest to turn the car around, he didn't have the heart to do it.

Pasting a smile on his lips, he hoped it looked natural. Hunter patted her hand, letting his fingers graze her soft skin. God, he loved touching her. "No, I don't want to go home, besides, I can't think of a better way to spend my evening than with a beautiful woman enjoying a fine dining experience."

Lila's grin widened, making her dark eyes sparkle. She leaned over and planted her glossy lips against his cheek. "Thank you. This means a lot to me."

A warmth spread throughout his body from the touch of her lips. "It's my pleasure. You look fantastic, by the way." And she did. Though he would have preferred her hair to be worn loose, it was pinned in a stylish topknot with loose strands framing her heart-shaped face. She didn't wear as much gunk on her face as the other women who'd flitted in and out of his life, yet none of them could hold a candle to her natural beauty.

Her dress was one of the items he'd purchased for her. A strapless jade gown which hugged her curves like a second skin. His cock stiffened with the mere thought of his plan to undress her when they got home. How he'd undo her hair to let it cascade around his shoulders. How he'd kiss every inch of her soft chocolate skin, until she cried out his name, begging him for more.

Hunter wasn't thrilled at the prospect of being in an uncontrolled environment. But he didn't want to disappoint Lila when he knew it meant so much to her to have a night out. That she didn't seem to mind she was spending it with him gave him the courage to see this thing through.

Her full lips curved to a smile. "And you don't look so bad yourself. You clean up rather nicely."

Hunter shook his head. "Just because I pay you a compliment, don't feel obligated to give me one back. We both know what I look like."

One finely arched brow shot up. "Oh? And since when did you become a mind reader? I happen to think you look very handsome right now. If you didn't have so many damn hang-ups, maybe you'd be able to accept what I say at face value rather than scrutinizing everything."

"What I accept is you're the kind of person who doesn't like to hurt people's feelings, but let's not try to sugarcoat this joke I call a face."

Folding her arms across her chest, she turned away from him. "I wish you wouldn't start this again, Hunter. I'm not interested in joining your pity party tonight."

"I'm not having a goddamn —" Realizing he'd raised his voice when he saw her flinch, Hunter paused. Taking a deep breath, he placed his hand on her thigh and gave it a light squeeze. "You're right. Learning how to accept myself as I am now is going to take some time, but I'll keep trying. For you."

Lila turned and faced him again, her dark brown gaze roaming his face. Hunter tried not to fidget under her penetrating scrutiny. Placing her hand on the scarred side of his face, she shook her head. "No. Do it for you."

There was no mistaking the sincerity in her voice. Lila Saunders was as genuine as they came, and he should have seen it right away. But he'd let his prejudices about women get in the way. Maybe he should let her go now instead of forcing her to spend time with him. But the moment the thought entered his mind, he immediately buried it again.

He'd have to let her go soon enough, but for now, he wanted to spend as much time with her as possible. Needed it. He enjoyed her company far more than he believed he would at the beginning of this arrangement. No, he wouldn't let her go just yet. Hunter intended to keep her with him for as long as he possibly could, even though deep down he knew it was wrong.

Dinner was every bit the ordeal Hunter pictured it would be. Besides the stares he drew in his direction, the minute they'd stepped into the restaurant, Hunter was aware of the hushed whispers and stunned gasps. He'd known this was what to expect, knew people would pause in the middle of eating and stare, some pretending not to, while others watched him openly.

Suddenly Lila released a groan. "Oh no."

"What's the matter?" he asked. Was she embarrassed being with him? She didn't seem to be at first but maybe he'd read the situation wrong.

"What's the matter?"

"It's my ex. He's here and he's coming this way."

Hunter frowned. "Your ex?"

Just then a good looking dark-skinned man stepped to the table. He had the kind of look that Hunter once possessed. This was Lila's ex? How could she be happy with someone like him if that was the kind of guy she used to date?

Lila glared at the newcomer. "What do you want Jason? I would have thought that since I didn't return any of your calls that you'd get the hint. We're done."

"You're just angry because I was with Veronica. It was just a stupid mistake."

"No, you were a stupid mistake, now if you'll please leave, I'm enjoying myself with my date."

Jason turned his attention to Hunter who willed himself not to flinch. He could see the shock on the other man's face as he caught a glimpse of some of his scars. "Are you serious?"

Lila crossed her arms over her chest. "As a heart attack."

"So is this why you've been ignoring my calls? I recognize him. He's that recluse property developer. Now I see why he doesn't come out in public much. I knew you were a bleeding heart but I didn't think you were into charity cases."

Hunter clenched his fists at his sides. He was itching to knock this motherfucker out but

"And this is exactly why we're finished. You are an arrogant jerk. You may be a respected physician but as a human being, you suck. You're a selfish piece of crap. Now do us both a favor and disappear and please lose my number. And if you continue to harass me, I will place a complaint with the medical board."

Jason glared before adjusting his tie. "Didn't realize you wanted to place out a real life beauty and the beast fantasy."

"Jason, you may think he's a beast because of the way he looks but you're ugly and rotten on the inside. Now be gone." She turned her back to Jason then and focused her attention on Hunter.

Lila ex stomped off in a huff.

"He seems nice," Hunter said with sarcasm.

"Don't let him get to you. It's good riddance to bad rubbish."

"He seem more your type," Hunter pointed out before taking a sip of his wine.

"Mean-spirited and self-centered? No thanks. I thought he was charming and sweet but as we dated I saw a different side of him. Then he gave me an ultimatum and I chose to break up with him."

"But it seems to be a letdown to go from someone who looks like him to someone like me."

"Stop it. I'm here with you and I'm enjoying your company. Just forget about that jerk. I already have."

It wasn't just what Lila's ex thought. It was everyone in the restaurant. What made matters worse was knowing what they were thinking. He could tell by the sympathetic stares some shot Lila's way. *What is that beautiful woman doing with that monster? He must be incredibly rich because she couldn't possibly be with someone like him.* And they wouldn't have been so far from the truth. What would they say if they knew he'd blackmailed her to be with him? They'd condemn him for being every bit the monster they believed him to be.

There was only so much of this he could take.

"Hunter." Lila stretched her arm over the table as she waved her hand in his face. "Earth to Hunter."

He shook his head to rid himself of the disconcerting thoughts swimming in his mind. "I'm sorry, were you saying something?"

"Can I go too?"

"What?"

"Wherever you were just now. I've been trying to get your attention for the last five minutes."

He was doing exactly what he promised her he wouldn't, feeling sorry for himself. *Come on, Hunter, you're being an ass. Pull yourself together.* Pasting a smile on his face, he gave her his undivided attention, determined to block out the curious glances thrown his way. "I apologize. I was thinking about how long it's been since I've been out like this."

"Are you enjoying yourself?"

"Of course. How could I not when I have the company of such a lovely companion?"

"You don't have to lay it on so thick, Hunter."

"It's true. You're gorgeous, and I think you know it."

She raised her shoulder in a nonchalant shrug.

"You don't give a damn about your looks do you?"

Lila shook her head. "Not really. I'd be lying if I said I didn't know I was attractive, but there are far more important things in life than being pretty. Eventually, my looks will fade and I'm okay with that because I have so much more going on in my life than my face. And I suspect you were the same way before your accident. You didn't give a damn about your looks before it happened, did you?"

It was on the tip of his tongue to deny it, but she was correct. Sure he knew what a good looking man he used to be, but he'd taken his face for granted. It was only now when he was deformed that it mattered to him so much. He twisted his lips into a half smile. "You never appreciate what you have until it's gone. What you say makes sense, but it's hard to not to be uncomfortable when people are staring at me like I'm a circus freak."

Lila sat back in her chair, crossing her arms over her chest, looking at him with a suspicious gleam of amusement in her eyes. Her glossy painted lips were slightly curved. Hunter didn't quite trust that look. He was beginning to learn what her expressions meant, and when the cogs were spinning. She was up to something.

"What's that look for?"

Her grin widened to reveal her even white teeth. "What look?"

"The one that tells me you're plotting."

She tossed her head back showing off the graceful column of her neck as she laughed. "I'm sure I don't know what you're talking about, Hunter. Has anyone ever told you you're paranoid?"

Hunter raised a brow. "When I'm given a good reason to be, I am." He stiffened at the feel of her stockinged foot easing its way up his leg. "What are you doing?"

Instead of answering, she picked up her fork and knife, cut a piece of asparagus and popped it into her mouth as if her foot wasn't sliding along his thigh.

Hunter's cock jumped to attention and her toes were mere inches from his crotch. Yet she sat across from as if nothing out of the ordinary was happening. "What are you doing?"

"You've already asked me that. I'm eating." She pressed the ball of her foot against his erection making him jump.

He inhaled sharply as heat rushed through his body. "Good God, woman, what are you doing to me?"

"Giving you something else to think about. Is it working?" She moved her foot against his cock in circular motions."

Hunter clenched the tablecloth between his fists as sweat broke out along his forehead. Not only was he no longer concerned about what people around them thought about his face, he doubted he'd make it ten minutes without fucking her senseless.

"You're asking for it," he said through clenched teeth, trying to hold on to his last bit of self-control.

Lila continued to stroke him with her foot, all while eating her meal as if nothing out of the ordinary was going on. When she put her fork down and winked at him, Hunter could take no more.

He yanked his cell phone from his breast pocket and punched in Ernest's number.

"Yes, Mr. Jamison?"

"Meet us out front in five minutes."

"Sure thing, boss."

Hunter clicked off and replaced his phone.

Lila pulled her foot away, a frown marring her forehead. "Why are we leaving?"

"You know why," he growled. Hunter pulled out his credit card to pay for their meal before signaling the waiter. "I think you know."

"But I'm not finished with my meal."

"You should have thought about that before you pulled your little stunt. Now, I'm going to finish what you started."

With their coats collected, and the bill paid, Hunter hustled her out of the restaurant in record time. He couldn't get her home fast enough to ease his aching hard-on.

Ernest had the car parked in front of the building as instructed. Wisely, the driver didn't ask questions about their dinner ending so abruptly.

Hunter held Lila against him, nuzzling her neck and inhaling the sweet scent of her fragrant skin. He gripped her thigh, pushing the hem of her skirt higher as he caressed her soft skin.

"Hunter, not here," she whispered, her eyes darting to Ernest, though she made no move to pull away from his caresses. In fact, she leaned into his touch, her body seeming to beg for more even though her mouth said otherwise.

"Payback is a bitch isn't it? All you have to say is stop and I will."

A whimper escaped her lips and Hunter knew he couldn't go another minute without tasting her. Lowering his head, he smothered her succulent mouth with his, plunging his tongue forward to sample her sweet essence.

With a sigh, she returned his kiss wholeheartedly, tangling her fingers through his hair and holding his head to hers. Not being able to touch her had been pure torture. He cupped her face to deepen the kiss, taking charge and showing how much he needed her. His body was on fire for her and his dick was so hard and sensitive it was almost painful to endure.

The ride home wasn't long, but Hunter didn't know how much longer he could hold out without being inside her hot, tight pussy. Kissing wasn't enough. He needed her. By the time they pulled up to the house however, Hunter didn't have the patience to make it to the bedroom.

He broke the tight seal of their lips only for a moment to leave instructions for his driver. "You can leave the keys in the ignition, Ernest. I'll pull the car into the garage when Miss

Saunders and I have finished talking." Talking was the last thing Hunter had in mind, but he knew his employee was too professional to say otherwise.

"Of course, Mr. Jamison. Have a good night."

Ernest slid out of the car and closed the door behind him with a decisive click. Once they were alone, Hunter pulled Lila across his lap with every intention of finishing what they'd started, but she placed her hands against his chest, halting the descent of his mouth on hers.

"Wait, Hunter. Shouldn't we go in?"

He ran his tongue over his lips to lick up the taste of her still clinging to them. "No. Remember, you started this."

"But in the car?"

He ran a finger along the top of her breasts peeking out of her dress. "Yes, in the car."

A gasp parted her lips and her shoulders shook with a shiver. "Ernest probably thinks we're depraved."

"He's not paid to think about what I do within the confines of my property. We're both consenting adults. What's the matter, sweetheart? Don't tell me you didn't mean it." Hunter buried his face against her neck. She trembled within the circle of his arms, but he could still feel her resistance. By the time he was finished with Lila, he would have her absolute surrender.

"Mean what?"

"You were obviously trying to get a rise out of me back at the restaurant and you got one. I'd hate to think you don't plan on following through."

"I do." She arched her neck, granting him the access he desired.

A smile curved his lips. Lila was weakening just as he knew she would. One thing he loved about her was how wonderfully responsive she was to his touch. The ways she'd shake at his every caress, moan and writhe against his passionate ministrations was enough to drive him to the brink of insanity. Nibbling on the soft flesh where her neck and shoulder met, he took his time exploring her creamy flesh before raising his head to meet her passion-glazed brown eyes. "Then what's the problem?"

"I was — oh! I can't think when you do that."

Hunter's hand slowly eased up her thigh, pushing her dress up as he made his way up. "Don't mind me. Finish your thought."

"You're infuriating, do you know that?"

"Mmm, so I've been told." He was more interested in getting her panties off so he could be inside of her, but he would humor her a couple minutes more. There was only so long she could hold him off. His concentration was on his task as he traced the fastening of her garter belt. "You were saying?"

"I was only trying to relax you when we were at the restaurant. I didn't mean for things to go this far."

"I see," he said solemnly, moving his hand higher until the tip of his fingers touched the edge of her panties. "Well, it certainly worked. I'm so relaxed, I can't think of anything other than fucking you, and you know what? I think I will.

She clamped her thighs together, trapping his hand between them. "Don't."

He raised a brow. "You don't want me to stop, Lila, not when I feel your heat. It's practically scorching my hand. I bet you're wet for me aren't you, darling?"

She averted her gaze as if she had something to hide. Hunter smiled, enjoying this game of cat and mouse, a game he fully intended to win.

"Hunter…"

"Open up for me, baby. Don't deny what we both want."

Her nibbled her bottom lip before slowly parting her thighs.

With her silent encouragement, Hunter grazed the crotch of her panties with his fingertips. "Hmm, just as I suspected, you're soaking wet. I think we're going to have to do something about that. Don't you think?"

She met his gaze once more with narrowed eyes. "Does it really matter what I think?"

"Of course it does. All you have to do is tell me to stop, but I don't think you want me to, do you?"

Clutching his shoulders, she hung her head in defeat. "You know I won't, although I didn't realize my actions would lead to vehicular sex."

"This is only the beginning, dear." He dipped his finger inside her panties and searched for her hot little treasure. When he grasped her clit between his thumb and forefinger, she bucked her hips forward.

"Hunter!"

"That's it, baby. Let it happen. Don't hold back. Admit it, Lila, this was exactly what you wanted when you did what you did."

"Mmm." She wiggled her hips against his hands. Lila didn't need to admit anything, because he already knew. Hunter had learned in the few short weeks they'd been together how Lila, though a very passionate and giving lover, was still basically shy when it came to vocalizing her sexual needs. She probably fooled herself into believing her attempt at seduction was to relax him, but Hunter was certain she'd done it as much for her benefit as for his. Lila wanted this as much as he did. The more time they were spending together though, she was opening up more and more.

Hunter released her clit and slid two fingers into her damp sheath, pushing them deep. "Your pussy is tightening around my fingers. You want it bad don't you, Lila?"

She ran her tongue across her lips, and nodded, her eyes tightly shut.

Chuckling, Hunter brushed his lips against the column of her throat. "You don't get off that easily. You're going to have to tell me how much you want this."

"You know…"

He slipped his fingers in and out of her, making her shake and moan. Hunter couldn't remember when he'd enjoyed a moment as much as this one. To have this gorgeous woman squirming on his lap, her cunt so wet and ready to be fucked… She was his for the taking and he couldn't wait to have her. But he'd have her admit it first. It was the least she owed him for the sexual torment she'd dealt out earlier.

"I do, but that doesn't mean I don't want to hear you say it. Tell me."

"I want you. Please. I need it. I need you. Don't tease me anymore."

Hunter had her where he wanted her. Debating on whether he should prolong her sensual torture, he decided against it. His rigid cock strained against his pants, threatening to break through. To continue teasing her as she deserved would have been just as hard on him if not more so. Besides, the evidence of her arousal soaked his hand.

Easing his fingers out of her tight cunt, Hunter brought them to his mouth and licked her juices off, never breaking eye contact with her. She watched him open-mouthed, her body trembling. Hunger lurked within the depths of her gaze as her tongue slid across her now bare lips.

He had to have her right here and right now. "Come here." Grasping her shoulders, he guided her until she straddled him with her knees resting on the leather upholstery. Her dress was hiked around her waist and her breasts hovered dangerously on the brink of popping out of the bodice clinging so tightly to her. Hunter grasped either side of her head with a groan and smashed his lips against hers.

Lila's mouth parted as her tongue darted forward to collide with his in a duel for sexual supremacy, but it was a battle Hunter fully intended to win. He held her head steady until he was satisfied in his exploration of the sweet recesses of her delectable mouth. Damn she tasted good, but once again, the ache of his groin reminded him of his other pressing need.

Tearing his mouth from hers, Hunter took a few gasps of air before softly commanding, "Undo may pants and take out my cock."

Lila opened her mouth as if she wanted to say something, but instead she merely nodded. Lifting her hips up just enough to maneuver her hands between their bodies, she fumbled with his belt buckle, unsuccessfully at first, but her second attempt was met with triumph. In hurried movements, she yanked down his zipper and slid her hand through the slit in his boxers.

When her fingers wrapped around his cock, Hunter felt as if he'd explode right then and there, silently praying not to come too soon. No, he wanted to save that for when he was inside of her. "Hurry!" So close to getting what he wanted, yet not quite, was driving him insane with a manic need.

Lila gently pulled his cock out of his pants and Hunter hooked his finger inside the crotch of her panties and pushed it aside. "Lower yourself onto me. Take every inch of me inside of you."

She positioned his dick against her wet opening before dropping her hips just enough for the head of his cock to enter her. "Hunter." The soft sigh of her voice was just enough to drive him over the edge.

With impatience, Hunter grasped her hips and surged up, sending his cock deep into her tight sheath. Wonder filled his being as he inhaled sharply. This wasn't the first time they'd fucked, but he still couldn't get over how right it felt being inside of her. How tight she was and how her muscles clenched so tightly around him. Most other times, he would have remained still for a moment to savor how absolutely perfect this feeling of being one with Lila was, but he was far too horny. There'd be time for that later.

Lila gripped his shoulders as she bounced her hips up and down, moving until his cock was nearly out of her and then going back down until he was so deep inside of her, Hunter wasn't sure where he ended and she began. His fingers dug into the tender flesh of her hips while he bucked his hips to meet her thrust for thrust. It took a few strokes to catch his rhythm, but soon their movements were so synchronized, it was almost like they'd practiced it many times before.

Having Lila here like this excited him like nothing else. The thrill of taking her, fucking her in a new location and her absolute surrender was a potent aphrodisiac he knew he'd succumb to any minute now. Gritting his teeth and willing himself not to climax just yet made his pulse race.

One of her breasts spilled out of her dress. Its dark nipple hardened as though beckoning him to taste, presenting a temptation he couldn't resist. This was how Adam must have felt when Eve presented him the apple, though Lila's offering was far more inviting. Leaning forward, Hunter captured the taut tip between his lips and sucked with desperate tugs. He couldn't get enough of her.

"Yes. Hunter. That feels so good."

Her moans egged him on as he explored the contours of her breast with his tongue, their bodies never missing a beat. She tasted so good, smelled so wonderful, felt so right. Releasing her nipple with a wet pop, Hunter raised his head with the intention of finding her lips. But something happened in that moment. Their gazes clashed and he saw something in her eyes, an emotion he couldn't quite make out, one he wasn't really familiar with, but it was a look that changed everything—shifted this joining of their bodies beyond mere fucking, to something much more profound.

Hunter couldn't put his finger on what it was, didn't have the courage to further examine it, but it happened nonetheless. The urgency suddenly left him, but the need increased. The longer they maintained contact, Hunter could tell, the same thing was running through Lila's mind. Slowly their mouths fitted together, and her arms went around his neck and her hands clasped the back of her head. Hunter held her against him knowing he must for no other reason than it was something he had to do.

They moved together, his cock still deeply imbedded in her pussy, their lips melded together as if it were their last kiss. He wasn't sure how long they stayed like that, but finally Lila was the one to turn her head away as she gasped, "I'm coming." Crying out, her head flopped back and forth and her shudders racked her body.

Hunter was close to his own orgasm, but the inner workings in his brain wouldn't allow him to speak. He shoved deeper into her, getting closer and closer to his climax until the buildup that had started in his toes moved along every inch of his body, throughout every limb, every fingertip and every nerve ending, resulting in something so powerful he shouted his release. "Lila! Lila! Lila!"

Shooting his load into her pussy, he held on to her so tight, never wanting to let her go, frightened that he'd never experience this almost spiritual feeling coursing through his soul again. Hunter buried her face against her neck. "Oh, God, Lila. I lo—loved it. That was…"

She nodded. "I know," she said with a whisper, holding on to him just as tightly as he was to her.

Hunter knew they should go inside. It was chilly out, but he wanted to stay like this just a little while longer. Lila didn't seem to be in any particular hurry to move either. What had happened here? Even if he was forced to put it into words, he couldn't. There was one thing he knew for certain: after tonight, things would never be the same between them again.

Chapter Twelve

Finally, the damn meeting was over and Hunter couldn't wait to get the hell out there. If he left now, he could make it home in under an hour.

Home to Lila.

The very thought of her brought a smile to his lips. Closing his laptop and shoving it into its case, he was ready to leave when Thomas walked over to him.

"Hunter, are you okay?" Confusion crinkled his friend's forehead.

The question took him aback. For the first time in a while, Hunter felt great. "What do you mean?"

"You've been walking around with this shit-eating grin all day. It's kind of creepy, man."

Usually a comment like this would have made him scowl, but nothing could rob him of his good mood today. Plans for the megaplex were going accordingly: in fact the new arrangements he'd proposed a couple months ago were working out better than he anticipated they would. His passion for his job had returned, but it was different. Hunter realized it was only just that. A job. And he wouldn't allow it to consume him as it had before. "Is there a reason why I'm not allowed to smile? It's a beautiful day."

Thomas narrowed his eyes. "Okay. Who are you and what have you done to Hunter Jamison?"

"Can't a man be happy for once?"

"But you're never happy."

Hunter should have been offended but he knew Thomas had a point. It made him feel guilty at how he must have come across to others in his depression. "Sheesh. You make me sound like a miserable bastard."

"I wouldn't be a good friend if I lied to you. I haven't seen you like this since..."

"Before my accident? Don't worry. You can say it."

"Now I know something's up. What's going on? First you come into the office whistling. Then, during our meeting not once did you halt Peter in the middle of one of his pompous tirades. Your tolerance is usually pretty low for his crap. To top it off, you're referring to your accident so casually. What's the deal with you?"

Hunter sighed. There was no point in keeping quiet. Thomas would get it out of him eventually anyway. He was also the only person who knew of Hunter's agreement with Lila because Thomas had wanted to know why he had pushed so hard to change the plans for the megaplex.

"Walk with me to my car." Hunter pulled his cell phone from his pocket and punched in Ernest's number.

The driver answered. "Are you ready, Mr. Jamison?"

"Yes. I'll be out in ten minutes."

"I'll have the car out front."

"Thank you." He flipped the phone shut.

"Okay, shoot," Thomas prompted.

"There's really not much to say other than someone special showed me what an ass I've been. It's never easy to change, but I'm trying."

Thomas adjusted his glasses on the bridge of his nose. "I've been telling you that for years, but you never listened to me."

"You never put it as eloquently as Lila."

Thomas's eyes widened behind his glasses. "Lila? As in Lila Saunders, the woman who could have cost this company hundreds of thousands, possibly millions of dollars? The very one you're practically blackmailing?"

Heat swamped his cheeks and Hunter was sure his face was bright red. He didn't care to be reminded of how he and Lila had come together. Deep down, he knew she wouldn't have looked his way had the circumstances not thrown them together, but the last two months of her stay had meant something to him. He liked to think she actually enjoyed being with him. Not once did she flinch when she looked his way, instead, she had a ready smile that seemed like it was just for him.

She continually sent his body into a tailspin like he'd never experienced with any other woman, and Hunter was glad to face a new day knowing Lila was a part of his life. His cock stirred as he thought of what he intended to do to her later tonight. A more passionate woman, he doubted he'd meet.

When Hunter had first met her, he'd only seen the surface, but as he got to know Lila better, he saw her inner beauty shined as bright as her outer shell. She was a rare jewel.

"Yes. The same one," he finally replied, tight-lipped.

"Don't get all defensive now. I've never seen you so over the moon, especially over a piece of ass."

Hunter halted in mid-stride and turned on the other man, baring his teeth. "If you refer to her as a piece of ass again, I'll knock your teeth in. Her name is Lila. Use it."

Thomas held up his hands. "Whoa. I meant no offense, and it's not more than what you yourself have called your other women."

"But she's not them."

"I guess she's not if you're getting so riled over her. I'm just saying."

"Saying what?"

"If you keep walking around with that dopey grin on your face, I may begin to think you're in love."

"I'm not—" Hunter broke off, wondering if there was any validity to Thomas's words. For so long he'd scorned that emotion, never seeing any proof of its existence. His mother, who seemed to throw that word around so freely, was on her fifth husband. Most of the married couples in his social circle were either bitterly unhappy or trying to put on a front for the rest of the world, while the others didn't bother to pretend.

Was what he felt for Lila more than just lust, friendship and companionship? She made him smile without trying and he missed her when she wasn't around. When she was with him, Hunter didn't want to let her out of his sight. Was that love? He wasn't sure. He didn't have the right to use that word in conjunction with her because in a month she'd leave him. The very thought caused him pain.

"Finish what you were going to say," Thomas interrupted his thoughts.

"I don't know. Look I have to get home, but I'll call into the office tomorrow so you can fill me in on how your meeting went with the Carver group." When he would have moved on, Thomas grasped his arm.

"Wait. I didn't mean to piss you off."

Hunter sighed. "You didn't. I'm just being overly sensitive."

"She must be a remarkable woman. Not only has she managed to tame the Beast, you've been wearing your hair tucked behind your ears. You didn't even turn your head when that jackass in the meeting kept staring at you."

Hunter hadn't noticed. Now that he thought about it, he hadn't dwelled on his scars in weeks. As a force of habit, he touched the imperfect side of his face. Maybe he was healing on the inside so much that the outside didn't matter as much anymore, another thing he had Lila to thank for.

"No. I suppose I haven't and yes, she is pretty special."

"Have you told her how you felt?"

"What do you mean?"

A knowing smile split Thomas's face. "I think you know. I'll talk to you tomorrow."

Hunter didn't bother to dwell on his friend's words. Ernest was outside waiting for him.

His driver hopped out of the car and opened the door for Hunter. "Good afternoon, Mr. Jamison. I trust your meeting went well?"

"Yes, thank you." He was about to get into the car when he remembered something important. "How are the grandkids by the way?"

In all the time the Coates had worked for him, he hadn't bother getting to know them, too wrapped up in his own world to even care. It was through Lila he'd learned more about his two employees in two months than he had in years.

Ernest's grin widened. "They're doing wonderfully. Mary is taking ballet classes, dances like an angel that one. Nathan is into soccer. As you know, his eighth birthday is coming up. I'd like to thank you again for giving Maddie and me the time off to attend."

"Anytime. Please don't hesitate to ask for time off when you need it. I think the two of you are due for a paid vacation pretty soon."

"You'll have a devil of a time convincing Maddie of that. She's not happy unless she's busy." Ernest chuckled. "Now let's get you home. I'm sure Miss Lila is waiting for you."

At the mention of Lila's name, he slid into the car. Usually, Hunter worked on his laptop on the ride home, but he knew he wouldn't be able to concentrate. Thomas's words came back to him. Did he love Lila? He went over it in his mind the entire way home.

When Ernest pulled the car to a halt, Hunter opened the door and got out, not bothering to wait for the engine to shut off. He hurried into the house and called out. "Lila!"

When he didn't get a response, he tore upstairs to the library where she spent a lot of her time. She wasn't there. His next stop was the kitchen. Maybe she and Mrs. Coates were chatting over tea? It amazed him how Lila had even made his normally stiff housekeeper unbend.

Mrs. Coates was there, but Lila wasn't. "Have you seen Lila?" he asked without greeting.

"Good afternoon, Mr. Jamison."

Suddenly remembering his manners, he grinned. "Good afternoon."

His housekeeper smiled. "Miss Lila was out back, the last I saw her."

"Thanks." He didn't stick around for her reply before heading out to the backyard.

Grinning broadly, he paused when he saw Lila running around the yard with the dogs. Her face was animated and she was laughing at Shadow and Deja's antics. She presented a lovely sight. He wondered if he'd ever get used to how lovely she was. Somehow, Hunter doubted it.

He saw she was wearing one of the new outfits she'd bought recently, a hot pink track suit. They had come to a compromise about her clothes. He had Ernest take Lila to her favorite department store to pick out anything she liked, which turned out to be mainly casual clothes. But at night she wore the items he'd selected for her. Hunter was glad he'd relented on that subject. She seemed happier because of it.

He observed her tossing a stick and the dogs running after it. Her face fell and a wistful look suddenly turned into a frown. Something was wrong. Hunter could feel it. His heart skipped a beat as he watched Lila maintain that sorrowful expression. Yes, something was definitely the matter.

"Come on, guys," she spoke to the dogs, "time to go in."

As the three made their way toward Hunter, Shadow and Deja noticed him first. They barked and then ran toward him in their excitement, tails wagging.

Lila's eyes widened in surprise at his appearance and then her smile reappeared, but it couldn't erase from his mind what he'd just seen. As she drew closer, he noticed her eyes were red. She'd been crying! He'd bet his last dime on it.

"Hi, Hunter. How did things go at the office?"

"They went well. Did you do anything exciting today?"

She shook her head. "Not really. Playing with the dogs has basically been the highlight of my day. You're home earlier than I thought you'd be."

Hunter raised a brow. "Is that a problem?

"Not at all." He studied her face for a moment. She seemed distracted.

Grasping her chin, he dropped a light kiss on her lips. "Are you sure everything is alright?"

She lowered her lids and nodded. "Lila, I thought we were going to be honest with each other. Tell me what's on your mind."

146

"It's nothing."

"I can't help if you don't tell me."

She nibbled on her bottom lip and looked as though she was debating on whether she could open up.

"Are you unhappy with me?"

Her head came up sharply. "No! You've been great company."

"So what's the problem?"

"I'm so used to keeping busy I'm going out of my skull. Plus I'm getting major cabin fever. I've only been out of this house a couple times since I've been here and it's wearing. I know what our arrangement is and I have no right to complain, but..."

Hunter felt like a jackass. Of course she'd get bored staying cooped up in his house all day. Why hadn't he thought to provide her with something to occupy her time? He'd been so caught up in his own needs, he hadn't dwelled on her. He had a nagging feeling she hadn't told him everything.

"There's more isn't there?"

"I miss my dad. This is the longest I've gone without seeing him. When I talked to him last night, he sounded happy actually. With the construction beginning, he's getting a lot of business from the workers who come in for lunch."

"But?"

"But I miss him and even though he says he's doing fine, I worry."

"Would you like to go home and visit him?" The words were out before he realized what he was saying, but there was no taking them back once he'd said them. When he saw the pure joy flit over her face, he knew what he had to do.

"Do you really mean that? You'd let me go home and see him?" Her eyes lit up and her face became more animated

147

than it had been in days. He hadn't realized how unhappy she was until this moment. So wrapped up in the joy she brought to his life, he hadn't stopped to consider how she must feel. Of course Lila missed her father; he was after all the reason she was here in the first place. And seeing how full of joy she'd become at the mention seeing her father, Hunter knew he couldn't deny her that pleasure.

"Yes."

Just as quickly as it had appeared, the light dimmed from her dark eyes all of a sudden. "I can't."

"Why not? I'll have Ernest drive you there."

"For how long though?"

He shrugged. "For a few hours I suppose."

Lila shook her head. "That's okay. It wouldn't be enough. I appreciate the gesture though."

Hunter's stomach lurched and it felt like it was twisting in knots. He knew the direction this conversation was heading but he found himself saying, "If you'd like I can arrange for you to spend a couple days with him." The thought of her being away from him even for that short period of time caused him pain, but he knew he had to offer because she wouldn't ask.

She caught her bottom lip between her teeth, and looked as though she was contemplating his suggestion before shaking her head again. "Thank you, but no. I have another month in our agreement. It wouldn't be fair to you considering how you've honored your end of the bargain. I need to do the same."

Her statement was like a sledgehammer to his heart. Did she only view the thing between them as mere duty? Just as he was beginning to suspect his feelings for her were so much more than sexual attraction she'd dealt him a painful blow. The sad part was: Lila probably wasn't aware of what she'd just done.

Had he been a fool to think she'd come to care about him a little? Did it even matter? Hunter had known things would eventually come to an end. If it truly made her unhappy to be here with him, how could he even justify keeping her? Sure they had a deal, but could he really live with himself knowing she was counting the days until she was out of here? He should never have thrown this offer at her in the first place. But now that he had, he'd have to deal with it. "It's okay. I don't mind. Besides, we can add two more days on if it makes you feel better."

With a smile she leaned forward and brushed her warm lips against his cheek. "You're a sweetheart, but seriously, I can hold out for a little while longer to see him. I'd much rather make the rest of our time together special."

Hunter wanted that too, more than he could ever put into words, but Pandora's Box had been opened and dammit, there was no closing it. Though it pained him to ask, he had to at least gauge if she felt something deeper for him than just the mere friendship she'd offered. "Lila, what are you plans for when you leave here?"

A brief frown flitted across her lips. "I haven't really thought about it, but I'll definitely spend a couple weeks with Dad and help him around the shop if it needs it, though I suspect he probably won't need much assistance in that arena. Then I guess I'll go back to work at the hospital."

"I see. Do you like your job?"

"I love it. I'm actually excited at the prospect of going back."

Hunter forced himself to get the words out for the next question. "Is there anyone special you left behind?"

"If I did, it would be over now considering what I've been up to these last couple months," she laughed. "Why?"

"Just curious. I find it hard to believe a beautiful woman like you would remain single for long."

149

Lila rolled her eyes. "You're not harping on looks again are you?"

"No. Just wondering." He took a deep breath. "Have you ever been in love?"

It took several moments of silence before she spoke. An unreadable expression entered her eyes he couldn't discern. Finally, she shook her head. "No. Once, I thought I was but I was wrong. Besides, I have had a knack for attracting the wrong kind of men."

Like myself, Hunter thought. Lila didn't deserve to be here with a bastard like him. She had a life to get back to and he was keeping her from it. What was the point in holding her for another month when she'd only end up leaving him anyway? It wouldn't be any less painful to let her go in four weeks than it was now. In fact each day that passed would cause him agony because he knew the day he'd have to let her go was drawing near.

Hunter stared into her lovely face, memorizing every line of her face, from the tilt of her chin to the curve of her lips. She was the definition of pure beauty. He knew what he had to do. His heart squeezed within the confines of his chest and it became difficult to breath.

Taking a deep breath, he said, "I guess you're probably wondering what's up with the twenty questions."

She grinned. "Well, it did cross my mind."

He scratched the back of his head. "Actually, I uh, didn't quite know how to broach the subject, before, but I needed assurance you had plans once you leave here. As it turns out, it'll be sooner than we both anticipated."

Her smile fell in an instant. "What do you mean?"

This was harder than he thought it would be, but he steeled himself to remain firm. "I mean go home to stay. I think it's time to bring this arrangement to an end."

Her mouth opened and her hand went to her throat. Judging from the stricken expression this wasn't good news, but surely he was misinterpreting her thoughts.

"Have you grown tired of me?"

If he wanted to do the right thing, he'd have to sever the ties right now while he still had the strength. "Don't take it personally, Lila. It's why I only asked for three months, because that's how long it normally takes for me to grow bored with the current woman in my life. I just didn't think it would happen with you so soon. Don't worry. I'll keep my end of the bargain. As a matter of fact, if you pack now, Ernest can probably get you home by dinnertime...unless you don't mind having one last quickie before you go."

Her jaw dropped. "How can you speak to me like this? You don't really mean it. I thought things were going well."

"Oh, they were. And I appreciate your company, but you knew as well as I, this would be ending. Better sooner than later, right?"

"How can you be so cold about the whole thing? I thought we were friends."

Hunter wanted to take her in his arms and kiss the hurt he saw lurking within the depths of her eyes. "We were friends...out of necessity. I would have said anything to gain your compliance."

Her lips thinned. "I don't believe you."

"Why not? Is it so hard to believe that someone could get tired of you? Now, who's the one hung up on looks? You're not as hot as you think, Lila."

"You son of a bitch," she whispered.

"I know." His lips curved to a smug grin. "But let's end things amicably."

Her hurt was then replaced by fury. Her fists clenched in front of her and for a moment he braced himself for a punch.

She didn't. Instead, the fire left her as soon as it had come and she dropped her hands to her sides. "All this time...I thought you were a good person, someone I liked very much, but you were having a good laugh behind my back. I was just another bed warmer to you. All those things you've shared with me in these past weeks have meant absolutely nothing. Have they?"

It had meant the world to him, Hunter wanted to shout, but now that he'd set on this course of action there was no turning back. "They did mean something. You were a great lay and for that I thank you. But you've also showed me that if one woman isn't repulsed by this mug of mine, I'm sure I can find another who won't be either. I simply have to go out and find myself another Pollyanna type."

She gasped.

Lila, I'm sorry. "Don't look so surprised, sweetheart. We had a good thing. Now it's time to end it."

"So it's true," she whispered.

Hunter frowned. "What is?"

"You really are a beast. You had me fooled. I believed I'd finally seen the real man aside from what the media portrays you as. But they had it right all along."

"I never pretended to be anything other than I am."

"No. I was the fool. But never again. Goodbye, Hunter." She hurried past him and if he wasn't mistaken, he saw her dark eyes shining with the suspicious gleam of tears.

When he heard the door slam behind her, indicating she'd gone back inside, his shoulders slumped. To say those things to her had been the most difficult task he'd done in his life. But deep down, Hunter knew he couldn't hold her anymore. He finally knew the meaning of the word love—letting someone go, even though it was killing you inside.

Chapter Thirteen

Lila stood to clear the plates off the table, but Mrs. Perez grabbed her hand. "Let me do that for you, dear. You've cooked this delicious meal, the least I can do is take care of the cleanup."

Her father nodded. "And I'll help. Gloria and I have sort of gotten into a little routine while you were away."

Mrs. Perez winked at Jesse. "I wash, you dry?"

"Of course." He grinned back.

Lila hadn't missed the meaning of the exchange. Those two had obviously gotten close in her absence. It seemed a lot of things had changed while she was gone. Her father was in the works of remodeling the store. His motto had been, 'If it ain't broke don't fix it, so it' so it had come as a surprise to see the beginning of the renovations.

Jesse had said Gloria and the teenagers who worked for him had suggested a few changes. Lila had been telling her dad for years about changing things around the store, so it surprised her that he'd been so open to the suggestion of others. Then she'd learned that Mrs. Perez had been over almost every night for dinner and in fact they'd gone out on several dates.

It seemed as if her father was doing well and thriving. He was losing weight, his blood pressure was low, and he seemed happy. Even being here right now made Lila feel like an intruder.

For so long it had been her and her father, depending on and taking care of each other, but having been away for two months, she realized her father was fine on his own. In fact, he seemed to be better off without her around.

"Okay," she finally answered. "I think I'm going to turn in a little early."

Jesse frowned. "Don't you want some apple pie? Gloria made it from scratch."

"Yes, please have dessert with us." Mrs. Perez smiled at her. Lila didn't doubt the other woman's sincerity, but she thought it best to leave the couple alone.

"I'll pass tonight, but please save me a slice."

After she left them alone, she went through the motions of getting ready for bed. When she was in the shower she let her head rest against the stall, the tears mingling with the water falling over her head. Her father was doing great, while the world around her was falling apart.

It was time she started to pick up the pieces of her life again. Perhaps she could contact the hospital and let them know she was ready to come back to work for them. Now would probably be a good time to start looking for a place of her own, especially when it was clear her father no longer needed her.

As hard as she tried not to think about him, her mind drifted to Hunter. What had started out as a sacrifice she was willing to make on behalf of her father turned into much more. She hadn't expected to like being with Hunter. Sexually, he fulfilled her as no one else had, satisfying her so thoroughly. Besides the physical however, they'd made a spiritual connection as well. Somewhere along the line, she began to care for him more than a little. He made her laugh, he engaged her mind, and she felt safe and secure in his presence. For so long she'd had to be strong, but in those weeks she'd been with him, Lila was able to relax her guard and let go of all her worries.

She realized that his words had had the power to hurt her because she had fallen in love with him. What a fool she'd been. She should have known what they had was doomed to end terribly. Not only were they from different worlds, he had too many damned hang-ups.

Still, it had taken her by complete surprise how he'd said such cruel things to her. It was almost as if he was trying to make her hate him. But that made no sense. By now, he probably would have moved on, so it was time she did so as well.

Later that night, as she tossed and turned in bed, Lila thought about Hunter. What was he doing now? Was he thinking of her? Did he regret the things he said? *Stop it, girl, he's not worth it.* And she refused to shed any more tears over someone who didn't deserve them.

She glanced at the clock, and saw that it was nearly midnight. Maybe a couple of sleeping pills and some decaffeinated tea would do the trick. On her way to the bathroom, to get the medication, she noticed the kitchen light was still on.

Lila frowned. Her father was usually in bed by now. Or had he forgotten to turn it off? Always conscious of the electricity bill, he wasn't likely to leave them on. After getting the bottle out of the medicine cabinet, she headed for the kitchen.

Her father was sitting at the table in his robe, sipping what smelled like hot chocolate in an oversized mug. There was another steaming cup across from him and instantly, she knew he'd been waiting for her.

She took the seat reserved for her. "How did you know?"

Jesse grinned. "The walls aren't that thick, baby. I knew it was a matter of time before you got up. I made your favorite.

Hot chocolate with cinnamon, whipped cream and a giant marshmallow. Just like when you were a little girl."

She smiled. "Thanks, Daddy, but I think I've outgrown this."

"You're never too old for my special hot cocoa. Anyway, it's the least I can do, especially when I see you're hurting. Do you want to tell me what's been going on?"

She squeezed her eyes shut. It was time to come clean. "I lied to you, Daddy."

"About your private nursing assignment? Yes, I know."

"What?"

"I knew almost from the beginning. First of all, it seemed like a major coincidence that shortly after you left for this so called job, I get a letter from Ramsey's stating they were no longer interested in buying my property. And then I get a phone call from you. You know I'm an old man and I don't mess with technology like you young people do, but I'm sharp enough to know about caller ID. When I saw that the call had come from an H. Jamison's house, I began to suspect what the deal was."

She lowered her head in shame. How stupid could she have been? She'd called from Hunter's house. Lila should have known her father would pick up on it, but she hadn't been thinking clearly. "Why didn't you say anything?"

"Because by the time I realized what was going on, it was too late to do anything about it. I'd hoped I misread the situation and it wasn't what I think it was."

"It was," she whispered, wishing she could have kept the details to herself, but she began to tell him everything, glossing over the most intimate of the details, but giving him a pretty fair picture of what had happened.

When she finished telling her tale, her father pounded his fist on the table, anger entering his eyes. "Dammit!"

"I'm so sorry. I shouldn't have lied to you, but I didn't know what else to do. Please don't hate me."

"Baby, I could never ever hate you." He scooted his chair next to hers and engulfed Lila in his embrace. She had no more tears in her, but being in her father's arms was a comfort.

"I shouldn't have lied to you."

"No. You shouldn't have, but my anger was directed to myself. When you were gone, I realized how much I had depended on you. I've said this time and time again, you're young, pretty and have a beautiful soul. You deserve a life of your own, not to have your world revolve around me. The very fact that you would do something like this shows me I should have been more firm about you getting out more and pursuing your own interests."

"Dad, you haven't been a burden to me. I love you."

"And I love you. But we both have our own lives to live and it's unfair of me to expect you to give yours up for me, and I won't let you anymore."

Lila finally found the courage to meet his eyes. "Are you disappointed in me, Daddy?"

"Honestly, I'm not happy about what you did. In the future, come to me before doing something that will affect me, okay?"

"I promise."

"Like I said, I've had a lot of time to put things into perspective. I've allowed my life to become stagnant. You and the shop have been my life and I don't believe that's been healthy. Lila, while you were away, Gloria and I have gotten close and I'm thinking about asking her to marry me. I know you may think I'm rushing things, but at my age, every day is a blessing."

"That's wonderful. I think you two are cute together."

He grinned. "You're not upset?"

"Not at all. She's a very nice lady, and I know she's been crushing on you for a while. At least one positive thing has come of this whole mess after all. If you two got married, would she move in here?"

"I haven't thought that far yet, but it would make sense with the store downstairs."

"Then I should probably start looking for another place to live."

"Honey, you will always have a home here."

"I know, but if or when you and Mrs. Perez get married, I don't think it would be a good idea for me to be around. You two will need some time to yourself. I know if I were recently married, I wouldn't want my grown daughter hanging around."

"Is there no hope for you and Hunter?"

Lila brought her head up sharply. His question took her by surprise. "What do you mean? He used me. I don't even want to talk about him."

"Are you sure? From what you've just told me, something doesn't quite add up. A man doesn't go from the way you described him to a jerk with the snap of the finger without there being a reason. Us guys aren't as complicated as you women."

"It doesn't matter. It's over."

"But you still love him," he said softly.

Lila sighed. "Dad, I don't want to talk about this anymore."

"Okay, baby, but you've always been a fighter. You always stood up for the little guy. I remember getting a call from your teacher when you were ten, and she told me you'd punched some little boy in the nose. When I came to pick you up from school and asked you why you did it, you looked me square in the eye and said, 'Because he was picking on the smaller kids'."

Lila laughed at the memory. She had been a bit of a firecracker back in the day. "What does that have to do with anything, Dad?"

"You seem ready to fight for anyone else, myself included, but when it comes down to you, you don't fight for yourself."

"Dad—"

He held up his hand. "Hear me out, baby girl. While I want to smash this Hunter character's face in for making such an indecent offer to you in the first place, I don't think he's as indifferent to you as you claimed he was. Something doesn't add up. And anyway, you still have feelings for him. Don't you think you owe it to yourself to find out the real reason behind his sudden about face?"

Her father might be on to something, but did she have the courage to put her heart on the line?

*

"This is getting ridiculous. You haven't heard a word I've said have you?" Thomas spoke loud enough to bring Hunter out of his daze.

Hunter tore his gaze away from the painting on the wall. He hadn't really been paying attention to much lately because his mind randomly wandered. "Huh?"

"Exactly. You can't go on like this."

"What are you talking about?"

"I think you know. You're letting your personal life get in the way of business again and this shit is getting old fast."

"What do you expect me to do about it?"

"Find someone else."

"I don't want anyone else."

Thomas rolled his eyes. "Then go to her, stupid. Get down on your hands and knees and grovel if you have to, but make things right. I'm tired of you sleepwalking through the office like the world is about to end."

"For me it did, but there's no going back. She wanted to go home. She was missing her father and what kind of bastard would I have been to make her stay somewhere she didn't want to be?"

"Did she actually say she didn't want to be with you?"

"No. She's too nice for that, but I could see it in her eyes."

"Is it possible you might have misinterpreted what you saw? She could have been missing her home, but it doesn't necessarily mean she didn't want to be with you."

"I don't know what to think anymore, but I know I shouldn't have held her because of that stupid agreement I made. But…"

"But what?"

"I was afraid of what she'd say when I told her how I really felt. I'm not sure if I would have been able to handle the rejection if I laid my heart on the line with her. With the other women, I got over it…but Lila, she's different."

"Because you love her?" Thomas asked softly.

"More than you can know."

"Obviously not enough."

Hunter shot his friend a glare. "What do you mean? Not being with her is killing me."

"If you really loved her, you would have taken that risk. That's what love is. I made that mistake once before and now it's too late for me, but it isn't for you."

160

"What the hell am I supposed to do? Go to her house and demand she love me back?"

"No, but you can go to her and tell her how you feel. At least you'll know one way or the other of her feelings for you instead of dwelling on what ifs. If she rejects you, then maybe you can move on with your life. Anything is better than the way you've been lately. I think I'd prefer the angry ogre over this show of apathy on your part."

Hunter swiveled in his chair wondering at the validity of his friend's words. Could he do it? Go to Lila? In all his life, he'd never met a woman worth laying everything on the line for, but Lila was well worth the fight. It was on the tip of his tongue to say so when they heard a commotion outside of his office.

"You can't go in there!" his personal assistant cried out.

It was déjà vu. Hadn't he lived this scene already?

His office door came crashing open, and Lila stood in the doorway looking so beautiful and as pissed as the first day he'd laid eyes on her.

"Mr. Jamison, I apologize for allowing this to happen again. She walked right past me. I'll call the police right away," Ann said from behind Lila.

"Call off your guard dog, Hunter." Lila's gazed was zoned on only him.

"Ann, that won't be necessary. I'm always available to Miss Saunders."

Ann looked as if she wanted to protest, but thought better of it. She shot Lila a glare before turning on her heel.

Hunter saw the smug expression on Thomas's face and he barked, "What the hell are you standing there for? Can't you see this is a private matter?"

Thomas grinned. "Of course. I trust you'll be more yourself the next time I see you." He nodded in Lila's direction before he left the two of them alone.

"And tell Ann to take messages for the next hour or so. I don't want to be disturbed," Hunter growled.

Thomas's smile widened. "Will do." He practically skipped out of the office.

Lila closed the door behind her and strode over to his desk.

Hunter schooled his features, hoping she couldn't read the turmoil raging within him. He wanted to take her in his arms and hold her close, but held back to see what she did. "To what do I owe the pleasure of this visit?"

She cocked her head to the side, her eyes narrowing to dark brown slits. "Is my showing up a pleasure?"

"Yes," he answered honestly.

She slammed her hand on his desk. "Then why the hell did you send me away the way you did? Were you telling me the truth when you said you were bored with me?"

"Lila, if I didn't know better I would think you actually cared." Hunter groaned inwardly. Now why the hell had he said that? He didn't want to drive her away again. "Look, I didn't mean that how it must have sounded."

"Then how did you mean it?"

"I don't know. My words get all jumbled up when you're around and I don't quite know how to act."

"Is that why you said those hurtful things to me? Because I'm not leaving here until I get the truth."

This was as good time a as any to lay his heart on the line. "When I saw how happy you were at the mention of going home, I knew I couldn't keep you with me anymore. It wouldn't have been right. And because I was too much of a coward to tell you how I really felt."

"And how is that?"

"I-I love you, Lila, I think I have since the moment I laid eyes on you, but I didn't know it then. Maybe it was lust at first sight but our time spent together meant so much more to me."

"You should have told me, Hunter."

"I didn't think someone like you would love someone like me back."

She placed her hand over her chest. "Someone like me? I'm just a person and I really wish you wouldn't place me on a pedestal. I'm not perfect. And someone like me would be honored if someone like you loved her." She walked over to his desk to stand in front of him. "During our time together, I'd come to love you, too. And I've spent the last couple weeks in hell trying to figure out why you would hurt me the way you did, because the man I came to care about wouldn't have done that."

"What?" Hunter wasn't sure if he'd heard her correctly.

Lila took a deep breath. "I said I love you, too."

Unable to contain himself any longer, he gathered her in his arms and ground his lips on hers, unleashing all the hunger that had been pent up over the last several weeks without her. Finally, he lifted his head. "Say it again."

"I love you."

Hunter rested his forehead against hers. "I'm sorry for the things I said. I thought I was doing the right thing by letting you go."

She pulled back just enough to slap him on the chest. "Don't you ever do that to me again! I will be the one to decide what's right for me."

He wrapped his arms tightly around her, not wanting to let go even if his life depended on it. "I won't ever do anything so stupid again. Please tell me this isn't a dream, my beautiful Lila."

"I hope it's not," she laughed through the tears streaming down her cheeks, "because if it is, I'm going to be pretty pissed."

Hunter grinned before burying his face against her neck, and inhaling her flowery scent. Having her in his arms again brought his body to life. His cock jumped to attention and he knew he couldn't go another second without having her. Raising his head, he looked deep into her eyes. "I need you. I can't wait."

Lila pressed her body closer, winding her arms around his neck and kissed his jaw line. "Neither can I but is it a good idea to—"

"No one would dare disturb us now." Not giving her a chance to say another word, he covered her mouth with his, relishing the way her soft welcoming lips seemed to fit so perfectly with his. Hunter had no idea how he'd managed to get through the past two weeks without her lying next to him.

He pushed his tongue past her lips to taste the heady flavor that was unique to only her. Lila returned his kiss with the enthusiasm of a woman starving. Good. That meant she wanted him just as badly as he wanted her. Too bad she was wearing so many clothes, but that could easily be remedied.

Breaking the tight seal of their lips, he fumbled with the buttons on her blouse until her top gapped open to expose her lace-covered breasts. Impatiently, Hunter pushed her bra up. Her nipples were already hard and they looked ready to be sucked. The sight of the hard blackberry-colored tips made his mouth water. "Gorgeous. I've missed doing this." Dipping his head, he took one hardened nub between his teeth and nibbled.

Holding his head to her chest, she wove her fingers into his hair. "Oh, Hunter, I missed you doing this to me."

He licked, laved and teased the taut point, making Lila moan deeply. Hunter loved how vocal she was. It told him how much she enjoyed his sensual ministrations although he wasn't sure of how much foreplay he could offer. He couldn't remember being this horny in a long time and he wanted nothing more than to fuck her bowlegged, to stave the frustration they'd both experienced the last couple weeks.

"More," she groaned.

Hunter raised his head with a smile. "You liked that?"

"Mmm, you know I do."

Chuckling lightly, he set his sights to her other nipple, giving it the same loving attention as he had the other. She tasted just as good as he remembered, but there was something he wanted more: some of that hot, tight, satisfying pussy of hers. Releasing the turgid tip with a wet pop, he moved to his knees as he dropped kisses against her belly. Hunter worked frantically to unfasten her jeans.

Lila offered him assistance, obviously as eager to get undressed as he was to undress her. Once he helped her out of her pants, her panties followed. Leaning forward, he placed a kiss against the patch of hair resting between her thighs. The scent of her arousal greeted his nostrils, making his cock harder than it already was.

Placing her hands on his shoulders to brace herself, she spread her legs in anticipation.

Hunter looked at her. "You're ready for it, aren't you?"

"You'd better believe it. I've spent too many sleepless nights fantasizing about this."

"Then I certainly hope the reality lives up to your dreams." He slipped his middle finger past her slick folds and into her tight cunt.

Lila inhaled sharply. "I have no doubt it will," she moaned, grinding her hips against his finger.

With his free hand he parted her labia before latching on to her clit. Eating Lila's pussy was such a turn on, he hoped he didn't shoot his load before he could get his cock inside of her. Hunter sucked on the engorged nubbin while sliding his finger in and out of her channel. She was so wet and ready for him, her juices rolled down the inside of her thighs.

"Hunter, I love it when you do that to me. It feels so good," she groaned.

He added another finger, shoving the digits deep into her hot hole. Lila cried out sharply, her hands gripping his shoulders tightly.

The grinding motion of her hips encouraged him to suck harder on her clit and finger her harder and faster. He loved the way she moved in rhythm with his touch and couldn't wait to be one with her again.

He continued to thrust his fingers into her until Lila began to shake. During their time together, he'd come to know her body well, and when she was about to orgasm. Slowly removing his cream-soaked fingers, Hunter began to lap at her pussy in anticipation of her climax.

When it came, Lila screamed his name. "Hunter!" Her nails dug into his shoulders and he was sure, had he not been wearing a shirt, she probably would have tore into his flesh. He licked her pussy and inner thighs, catching her juices on his tongue.

She leaned forward as if her legs were going to buckle, but Hunter was ready for her. Catching her in his arms, he eased Lila on her back.

With frantic motions, he unbuckled his belt and was out of his pants in five seconds flat. His cock strained against his boxers to the point of pain. Hunter made short order of those as well. He didn't bother to take off his shirt. The sooner he could be inside of Lila, the better.

With a smile on her face, offering wicked delight, she spread her legs, and held out her arms to him. "Hurry, Hunter."

Needing no further encouragement, he positioned himself between her thighs. Grasping his cock he guided the rock hard shaft to her pussy. He ran the tip along her slit before pushing himself into her.

Hunter gasped as he sunk balls-deep into her. "Jesus Christ," he hissed between clenched teeth. Her pussy gripped him in a vise, sucking him deeper still. She was so damned tight and it felt right as if the two of them were made for each other. Planting his hands on either side of her head so his arms could hold him braced, Hunter remained still for a moment simply to savor this moment.

What a fool he'd been to let her go. They belonged together. She was his.

He glanced down at Lila, to see her eyes closed. A smile curved her full lips and he could tell she was enjoying the sensation of being deliciously stuffed with his cock. Bending his head, he dropped a light kiss against those luscious lips of hers.

Lila opened her eyes with a smile. "I love you, Hunter, but I'd love you more if you finished what you started."

Hunter threw his head back and laughed. "What Lila wants, Lila gets."

"And don't you forget it."

He moved slowly at first to find his rhythm, and then began to pick up the pace. Lila lifted her hips to meet each thrust and clenched her muscles even tighter around his cock. Hunter knew with absolute certainly he wouldn't be able to hold out long, but he intended to revel in every moment of it.

Hunter positioned his upper body on his forearms, enabling him to kiss her more easily. Lila wrapped her lithe legs around his waist, her eyes locking with his. Cupping the back of his head, she guided it towards hers until their lips met. Their tongues dueled as they strained together in a dance as old as time.

His balls tightened signaling his climax was near. Gritting his teeth, he tried to hold on, wanting Lila to come first. Fortunately he didn't have long to wait before her legs tightened around his waist and she cried out release. Finally he let go. With a loud grunt, he came, shooting his seed deep into her pussy.

Panting he rested his head against the curve of her shoulder. Never had he been so overwhelmed with emotion. He felt so many things for this amazing woman, love, pride, and contentment, not to mention happiness.

"I love you, Hunter Jamison," she whispered.

Hunter's heart leapt in his chest. There was no feeling in the world like loving someone and being loved back. For so long he'd scorned the emotion called love, but no longer would he doubt its existence because he found his soul mate in Lila. "I love you too. More than you can know."

Without warning she began to giggle. "Do you think they heard us outside? Your assistant's desk isn't that far from the door."

Hunter smiled. "I don't give a damn. It's no one's business what I do with my woman."

"Am I really your woman, Hunter?"

"Damn right." He kissed the tip of her nose. Hunter wanted to pinch himself to verify this wasn't a dream. "I can't believe this is happening, that you actually love me—especially when I look like this."

She ran his fingers along his scars. "All I see is a handsome prince."

The sincerity in her words could not be denied. "A prince needs a princess. I want you to be her."

Lila raised one delicately arched brow. "Are you asking me to marry you, Hunter?"

"No. I'm telling you. After making the mistake once, I'm not going to do it again. I can't take back the nasty things I said, but I can spend the rest of my life making up for them."

She threw her arms around his neck and he held her tight. Nothing ever felt so right.

The Beast had finally captured his beauty. And this time, it was forever.

About the Author

New York Times and USA Today Bestselling Author Eve has always enjoyed creating characters and stories from an early age. As a child she was always getting into mischief, so when she lost her television privileges (which was often), writing was her outlet. Her stories have gotten quite a bit spicier since then! When she's not writing or spending time with her family, Eve is reading, baking, traveling or kicking butt in 80's trivia. She loves hearing from her readers. She can be contacted through her website at: www.evevaughn.com.

More Books From Eve Vaughn:

A Night To Remember

Whatever He Wants

Dirty

Run

The Auction

GianMarco: Blood Brothers Book 1

Niccolo: Blood Brothers Book 2

Romeo: Blood Brothers Book 3

The Kyriakis Curse

Made in the USA
Monee, IL
23 March 2022

93429976R00095